Maureen,
Hope you really
enjoy the saga of
Buckey Bob and the
DIGFFL. Welcome to
the Brotherhood (and
Sisterhood) of the
pigskin.
Best,
Wade

Maureen,
thanks for the great
friendship over the years.
Welcome to the
Brotherhood of
Football. Enjoy the
book.
Mike

Brotherhood of the Pigskin
A Fantasy Football Novel

by

Wade Lindenberger

&

Mike Ford

iUniverse, Inc.
New York   Bloomington

Brotherhood of the Pigskin
A Fantasy Football Novel

Copyright © 2008 by Wade Lindenberger and Mike Ford

All rights reserved. No part of this book may be used or reproduced by any means, graphic, electronic, or mechanical, including photocopying, recording, taping or by any information storage retrieval system without the written permission of the publisher except in the case of brief quotations embodied in critical articles and reviews.

This is a work of fiction. All of the characters, names, incidents, organizations, and dialogue in this novel are either the products of the author's imagination or are used fictitiously

iUniverse books may be ordered through booksellers or by contacting:

iUniverse
1663 Liberty Drive
Bloomington, IN 47403
www.iuniverse.com
1-800-Authors (1-800-288-4677)

Because of the dynamic nature of the Internet, any Web addresses or links contained in this book may have changed since publication and may no longer be valid. The views expressed in this work are solely those of the author and do not necessarily reflect the views of the publisher, and the publisher hereby disclaims any responsibility for them.

ISBN: 978-0-595-51391-8 (pbk)
ISBN:978-0-595-50676-7(cloth)
ISBN: 978-0-595-61878-1 (ebk)

Printed in the United States of America

ACKNOWLEDGMENTS

Thanks to the many friends and family members who generously read the early drafts of this book.

Thanks to the long-time members of the IJGFFL. Their one-of-a-kind personalities inspired us to write this book.

Finally, thanks to our immediate family members - Kayoko and Max Lindenberger and Anne, Andrew, Daniel, Elizabeth and Carolyn Ford for their support and for encouraging us to write this book.

PREGAME SHOW

A Budweiser truck barrels down south Willow Glen Drive toward its next delivery at Cottonwood Golf Course, the driver asleep at the wheel despite a Tim McGraw song blaring out of the radio. Left to its own devices, the truck drifts into oncoming traffic.

The northbound driver of a maroon Chevy pickup notices the erratic Bud truck and compensates by swerving right. The Chevy's horn sounds a loud warning. It does its job, rousing the Bud truck driver from dreams of touchdowns and NFL cheerleaders. He corrects the truck's course, just missing the Chevy.

Meanwhile, a late-model, silver Lexus turns left from Corte de las Piedras onto Willow Glen Drive just as the Chevy and the Bud truck swerve to avoid each other. The Lexus driver sees the Bud truck rushing headlong toward him and jams the car into reverse, causing him to collide with the maroon Chevy.

KICKOFF

The year was 1990. Macaulay Culkin was left home alone. Laura Palmer got killed. *Goodfellas* played in theaters across the nation. The supermodels—Linda, Christie, Naomi, Tatiana, and Cindy—took over MTV in George Michael's "Freedom 90" video. Claudia Schiffer hawked Guess? jeans. Julia Roberts played *Pretty Woman*. The Fresh Prince (Will Smith) came to TV. *In Living Color* cracked up America with the Wayans brothers, Jamie Foxx, and Jim Carrey.

Millions of people experienced the bizarre fantasy world of Tim Burton and Johnny Depp in *Edward Scissorhands* and the bizarre *real* world of Marion Barry, the crack-addicted mayor of Washington DC. Roseanne Barr butchered "The Star-Spangled Banner" and got booed out of San Diego Stadium. On the political front, George Bush Sr. rode high in the saddle as the Gulf War got underway, the Soviet Union collapsed, and East and West Germany reunified.

In football, the San Francisco 49ers, led by the MVP performance of Joe Montana, trashed the Denver Broncos in Super Bowl XXIV in the Crescent City, New Orleans, by a lopsided score of 55–10.

In the San Diego office of Jenkins & Turner (J&T), one of the largest international CPA firms, the information systems (IS) consulting practice was cranking out the highest billable hours and revenue in the nation.

It was early August 1990 and football season was on the way. Robert Barrymore, the architect and leader of the J&T IS practice nicknamed Ladies' Man because of his self-professed skill with the opposite sex, reclined in his large corner office in his custom black leather chair reading the *Sporting News* and boning up on college and pro football.

Bernie Gregory, one of the charter members of the J&T IS practice, appeared in the doorway. "Hey, Ladies' Man, you got a minute?"

"For you, Bernie, sure. What's up?"

"I've got an idea to make the football season a little more exciting."

Robert put down his paper, giving Bernie his full attention. "You got lap-dancing cheerleaders lined up?"

"No, not quite that good. Have you heard about this thing called fantasy football?"

"I have indeed."

Bernie paused a second, a big smile spreading across his face. "I think we should start a league of our own."

"You do, huh?"

"Yeah."

"I don't know. It's a lot of work for *someone*. Keeping those stats and calculating scores."

Bernie scratched his head, thought for a second, and replied enthusiastically, "I can do that. It's no big deal."

"Are you sure about that? You're going to have to scour the newspaper every week to tally the scores and fax the results to everyone. And you know this group. Everyone's going to whine and complain no matter what you do. It'll be more like being a den mother in the Girl Scouts than anything else."

"Yeah, I know, but I think it'll be fun to kick your ass on a weekly basis. Plus, it'll give me something to brag about on Monday morning."

Ladies' Man raised an eyebrow in quiet derision. "Suit yourself. And who's gonna be in the league?"

"Basically the guys who are going on the Vegas trip. You, me, Junk, Chet, Exacta, Bob DiGiorgio, Marty Tanaka, and Gerald Phipps. That's eight, a good, even number to set up a schedule. And we can do the draft while we're there. It'll be perfect."

"Could work. So you'll set it up?"

"I'll check with the others and take care of everything."

"Sure. Why not?"

Las Vegas was the perfect place for the inaugural draft. Ladies' Man often took trips to Las Vegas with his buddies to play golf, drink, gallivant, and gamble. He had already organized one such trip for the weekend before the NFL season kicked off, inviting the men who would comprise the original members of the new league. A Vegas sports bar was the right environment for the draft, with half-naked women, the smell of money, and free booze. The seeds for a perfect day of golf, gambling, and fantasy football were planted.

THE FIRST QUARTER

When the group arrived in Vegas early Sunday morning and checked in at Caesars Palace, Ladies' Man immediately located the sports book to place bets on several NFL preseason games he had been tracking. He bet on just about everything, including the over, the under, the parlays, and bets like who would score the first touchdown in the Cowboys versus Redskins game. After placing his bets, he rounded up the entire group, and they hunkered down in the sports book to watch the forty TV screens and follow the progress of all of their bets.

The team owners were slated to convene for the draft in Ladies' Man's soundproof, deluxe suite at about 7:30 PM. The suite had everything, including a fully stocked bar, four large color TVs strategically placed throughout, and a dining room table large enough to accommodate all of the team owners.

Ladies' Man, resplendent in a red velvet smoking jacket, was reclining with a snifter of Courvoisier in a leather easy chair when he heard a knock on the door.

"Room service."

Ladies' Man opened the door to a beautiful brunette, not more than twenty years of age. She pushed a room service cart chock full of buffalo wings, chips, salsa, pizza, and mini cheeseburgers. Behind her was another cart with steak sandwiches, fries, and onion rings.

After scanning the food, his eyes rested on the young woman's name tag. Conveniently located just above her ample right breast, it said "Roberta."

"Come on in, Roberta."

"Thank you, sir. Where shall I put this?"

Ladies' Man walked over to the large window overlooking the Vegas Strip.

"Right here, darlin', if you don't mind."

As Roberta busied herself setting up the carts and unwrapping the food, Ladies' Man admired the smooth lines of her butt through her tight black skirt and wondered if she was wearing any panties.

"Very nice," Ladies' Man murmured quietly.

Roberta turned around, a little smile crossing her lips. "Sir?"

"The food. It's very nice. Looks extremely tasty."

"Yes, sir," her smile widened as she returned to the food. After setting out the condiments and utensils, Roberta removed a bill from her apron and walked over to Ladies' Man.

"Here you are, sir. Will you be charging this to your room?"

"Yes I will, Roberta. Yes I will. And here's a little something for you."

Ladies' Man removed a hundred-dollar bill from his pocket, folded it lengthwise, and grinned mischievously. "Where shall I put this?"

Roberta's eyes lit up when she saw the sawbuck. After a moment, she said, "You can put it right here," reaching out her hand.

"Sure thing, darlin'. Say, we're having our fantasy football draft up here, but it should be over in about two hours. I've got a full bar and champagne on ice. What say you and I do a little celebrating after that?"

Roberta sauntered up to Ladies' Man, touched his cheek lightly, and said, "I'm tempted, but my husband just got out of prison, and he's expecting me home when I get off work. I think he might be a little upset if I don't come straight home. You understand, don't you?"

"Holy shit. What was he in for?"

"Assault."

L-Man's eyes widened as Roberta nodded and inserted the hundred-dollar bill into her bra, sashaying out of the suite. Ladies' Man watched her exit with a sigh.

The team owners straggled in at various intervals. After obliterating all of the food, they took up places at the dining room table, pushing aside beer cans, shot glasses, and dirty plates.

Bob DiGiorgio, an Ohio State grad who everyone referred to as Buckeye Bob, sat cross-legged on the floor with newspapers, magazines, green-bar computer paper, and several empty Lite beer longnecks strewn around him.

"Damned if I know where to start," he said. "I think I want a quarterback first, but it seems like running backs might be the best way to go. Hell, I don't know."

He pushed aside the debris and studied his player rankings.

Across the room, Marty Tanaka, nicknamed Cactus Connection because he hailed from the Arizona desert, harangued Bernie Gregory, who had come up with the rules and set the schedule for the inaugural season. Bernie stood silently, a tight smile on his face. Marty was lost in his rant and might as well have been talking to the wall. Every time he flailed his arms to make a point, Jack Daniels slopped out of his highball glass.

"I've been looking at this scheme for scoring the defense that you pulled out of your ass," Marty said. "How the hell is anyone supposed to figure out how to pick a team with all the variables? I mean, shit. Points scored, including special teams, yardage, fumbles, interceptions, touchdowns scored, and safeties. What a fucking hodgepodge of absolute shit."

"Are you done, Marty?" Bernie said.

"Huh? No. And what about the tiebreaker? What a piece of unadulterated crap that is. Who ever heard of using the total bench score to break a tie? You have your head up your ass."

Bernie, no longer smiling, waited a moment to see if Hurricane Marty had subsided. Apparently it had.

"Look, Cactus Head, we talked about all of this when I put out the first draft of the rules. You had plenty of chances to bitch about this, and guess what? You didn't say shit. As the honorable and gracious interim commissioner of our fledgling league, I advise you to shut the fuck up and take it like a man."

Marty muttered something unintelligible and wandered away to top off his Jack Daniels.

As draft time neared, Bob gave up trying to come up with a strategy and joined Gerald "Slowhand" Phipps in a game of shotgun. Slowhand, a rabid Eric Clapton fan, had brought a funnel and a large length of rubber tubing. Inserting the funnel into one end of the tube and holding the other end of the tube up, Bob poured beer into the funnel. In all, he fit in four beers before the funnel filled up. Slowhand readied himself and tipped the open end of the tube into his mouth, opening his throat and letting the beer flow unobstructed. Bob stared at Slowhand in amazement as he drained all forty-eight ounces.

"Damn. Five point five seconds! That's fucking incredible!"

Slowhand sucked air like a beached fish, trying to catch his breath.

"Hot damn. That was a rush! A couple more of those and I'll really be fucked up."

Bob grabbed the empty apparatus from Slowhand.

"Okay, my turn. Grab the margarita pitcher and start loading this sucker up."

"You gotta be shittin' me. The hard stuff?"

"Damn right. Beer is for pussies. I wanna get higher."

"Whatever you say, Bob."

Bob polished off the margaritas just as Ladies' Man convened the draft.

"Alright, boys. Welcome to the first annual J&T fantasy football league draft. I'm looking forward to an exciting year and some good old-fashioned smash mouth competition. Our esteemed colleague, Bernie, has graciously volunteered to run the league and tally the scores this year, so I'm going to turn it over to him for some last minute instructions."

Bernie stepped up and shook L-Man's hand.

"Thanks, Robert. Time to kick this thing off. We already faxed you the draft order, but for those of you who are impaired in some way, it's Buckeye Bob, Ladies' Man, Slowhand, Bernie, Junk, Exacta, Chet, and Marty. I also faxed you the draft sheets. We pick one through eight, then turn back around, the guy on the end getting two picks, until we each have twenty players. Should be pretty simple for most of you. Any questions?"

Marty raised his hand.

"Yeah, Marty?"

"Who the fuck set the draft order? Did Price Waterhouse observe it to ensure its integrity?"

"Yeah, we hired Price Waterhouse. They will also present the awards at the end of the year. Any other questions?"

Lance Billings, also known as Junkyard Dog or just plain Junk, commented, "What if someone's hurt and the guy drafting doesn't know? What's the protocol on that?"

"Good question, Junk. This is a gentleman's league."

Everyone stared at each other, confused by the use of the word "gentleman" to describe this league.

"Yes, that's right. If you know someone's hurt or has been suspended for addiction to heroin, it is your duty as a gentleman to let the team owner know so he has the option of making another selection. Okay? More questions?"

Marty launched his highball glass against the far wall.

Ladies' Man shook his head. "We'll put that on your tab, Cactus Knob."

Marty flipped off Ladies' Man. "I got one more question, for Bernie. You're a dickhead."

"Hey, Marty, that's not technically a question, but I realize you wouldn't understand that, since you dropped out of school after the fourth grade, so I'll let it slide this time. Let's get this sucker rolling! Bob?"

Everyone turned their attention to Buckeye Bob, who was fumbling with the empty beer bong. "Huh? Oh yeah. Ah, shit, how does this thing work again?"

"Bob, you've got the first pick. What'll it be?"

"Okay. Um. I've got it down. Just a second here. I know where it is."

Bob rooted through the pile of newspaper and came up with a page with a big red circle in the middle. "Let's see. I can't read this goddamn thing."

He put the paper right up to his nose, squinting.

"That's what it says. It's gonna be a goddamn Brown, I tell ya. My first pick is Bernie Kosar!"

Marty reacted first.

"Wow, that's a good one, Buckhead. Add Metcalf, Slaughter, and the Browns' defense and you should average fifteen, no wait, twenty points a game. Go back and have another margarita. Your season's over before it even started."

The draft proceeded slowly, the team owners feeling their way, trying to get used to the vagaries of fantasy football. They selected household names like Barry Sanders, Eric Dickerson, Sterling Sharpe, Jerry Rice, Joe Montana, and Dan Marino, along with short-lived stars such as Christian Okoye, Don Majkowski, and Jim Everett.

Ladies' Man seemed to have the draft down from the beginning. He boldly selected Warren Moon second and emerged with a formidable starting lineup that included Thurman Thomas, Marcus Allen, Andre Rison, and Gary Clark. He was the odds-on favorite going into Week One.

The party raged into the early hours, and Ladies' Man said goodnight to Slowhand and Buckeye Bob at 2:30 AM.

"Get some sleep, boys. Remember, we got a big golf match tomorrow."

Buckeye Bob dismissed Ladies' Man with a wave of his hand. "Fuck that. We're hittin' this all-night strip club. I think it's called the Pink Lady or something like that. You should come with us."

"Nah, I think I'll get some sleep."

Slowhand slapped Ladies' Man on the arm.

"Aw, come on, old man. Let's go have some fun."

That did it for Ladies' Man. He always rose to the challenge, and no one was going to call him "old man."

"Get on your drinking hats, boys. It's show time."

On day two of the Las Vegas outing, the group headed out to Las Vegas National, home of several past PGA tournaments. Ladies' Man, feeling no pain from the previous evening, also felt pretty good about his game, so he orchestrated a number of side bets among the eight golfers, collecting $125 from each and volunteering to administer the results. Ladies' Man and Buckeye Bob were matched up as partners on one of the team bets, a good pairing because Bob provided a steady and conservative contrast to Ladies' Man's high-risk approach to the game.

As they stood on the first tee, Ladies' Man gave Bob a pep talk.

"Now, Buckeye, I don't wanna put any undue pressure on ya, but we got a lot of money riding on this. And to be honest, you got me kind of worried yesterday, bettin' on the Browns and drafting so many of their players and all. I mean, I know you're from Ohio and all and they're your team, but jeez, those guys reek and there are limits. Bernie Kosar? Come on. Bottom line, I think your judgment's a little suspect."

"Don't worry about me, Ladies' Man. I'm solid. I got ya covered."

"Good man. For a Buckeye that is."

Buckeye Bob wasn't a J&T alumnus. He had come to the group after becoming friends with Bernie and Ladies' Man through the CPA/ attorney over-the-line softball and basketball tournaments they had played together over the years. He had worked for North and Sullivan, one of the other giant international accounting firms. Bob joined North and Sullivan's Cleveland office after earning his bachelor's degree in accounting from Ohio State University. He loved Cleveland, but when he got a chance to transfer to sunny San Diego, he jumped at it.

Ladies' Man and Bob had a great front nine and felt they had a shot at a good share of the winnings despite their numerous visits to the drink cart for beer with whisky chasers. As Ladies' Man neared the twelfth tee, he pulled out Big Bertha, the club that he pressed into action when he wanted a long drive. Ladies' Man grasped the club and stated, "Gentlemen. It's time to let the big dog eat" as he stepped up to the ball.

The twelfth hole, a 423-yard par four, doglegged slightly left, with water on the right side of the fairway. Like the other holes on the course, the backyard fences of the houses lining the fairways marked the out-of-bounds area, in this case on the left. Ladies' Man sized up the situation and took a massive cut. The ball appeared to be headed toward the corner of the dogleg, position A. However, as it landed, it hit the cart path and took a wicked hop to the left, toward the houses. Ladies' Man and Bob jumped in the cart and tore down the path to locate the ball, circling the area for a few minutes until Bob spotted the ball on the other side of the fence.

Ladies' Man eyed the ball for a minute. As he began to walk toward the fence, Bob heard him say, "Damn it, that's my lucky ball. I'm not letting any damn fence get in my way." He proceeded to scale the steel fence to retrieve it. As he reached down to pick it up, he heard

Bob yell, "Dog!" Ladies' Man looked up. A huge, pissed-off rottweiler confronted him. Ladies' Man began to speak to the dog in a calm, measured slur, but the dog eschewed conversation. Ladies' Man turned and raced to the fence, pursued by the rottweiler. As he scaled the fence, the dog jumped with him and bit his pant's leg, taking a hunk of flesh in the process. Ladies' Man cleared the fence, did a barrel roll, and landed upright. Bob rushed over, expecting the worst, and found Ladies' Man grinning, the ball held up between thumb and index finger, none the worse for wear.

"Jeez, L-Man, you're bleeding. Look at the chunk that dog took out of your leg."

"Thass okay, Bob. I've got a first aid kit and some really good painkillers in my golf bag."

Ladies' Man finished the round with the same ball, a bloody leg, and numerous winnings from the skins game and the team bet with Bob. Later that evening, they used the victory money on the craps table and almost tripled their money.

As the group drank one last round in the hotel bar before heading to the airport, Bernie floated a couple of ideas he had been pondering since they decided to start the league. "Guys, this new league is great, but it needs a name."

Chet Russell, another long-time member of the J&T crew, chimed in with, "How about the Pompous Ass Fantasy Football League, or PAFFL for short?"

Junk offered up his opinion next. "I like DIGFFL. Drinking is Good."

Of course, Ladies' Man couldn't resist. "It should be WIGFFL. Women is Good."

"Don't you mean, women are good?"

"Whatever."

Bernie waved them off. "I was thinking BIGFFL."

Perry Comstock, nicknamed Exacta because of his passion for betting on the ponies said, "That's pretty cool. Does BIG mean large, important, that kind of thing?"

"No. It means Bernard I. Gregory."

A chorus of catcalls and boos went up.

"Yeah, yeah. And since I've taken on the duties anyway, I also propose that I be awarded the ceremonial title of commish."

More jeering.

Marty Tanaka offered, "How about fuck-face or douche bag?"

Bernie ignored him. "All those in favor of BIGFFL raise your beers."

Everyone raised their beers.

"Done. Here's to the BIGFFL."

As expected, in the inaugural BIGFFL season, Ladies' Man won the championship going away. In August 1991, Bernie "The Commish" Gregory began gearing up for season two. In the previous few weeks, Bernie had received numerous communications from the owners, requesting something closer for the second season.

His message light blinked rapidly, so he took a short break from preparing for a client meeting to check his voice mailbox on the off-chance that a non-BIGFFLer had called. Just as he suspected, he had yet another message from an owner, this time Junkyard Dog, who could have walked the twenty-five feet to his office, but liked to leave epic, impassioned voice mails instead. The moment he heard Junk's strident voice, Bernie hit delete and sent the message into space, never to return.

Unable to concentrate, Bernie got up to stretch his legs, picking up the baseball he treasured, signed by Juan Marichal, Willie McCovey, and Willie Mays. Just for kicks, he also put on his San Francisco Giants hat he kept on top of his bookshelf, transporting himself back to the days when, as a kid growing up in San Jose, he was a huge Giants fan. He spent many a summer night watching McCovey, Mays, Marichal, Alou, and his other heroes. He had so wanted to be one of them some day, and for a time he thought his dream would come true. However, in his senior year of high school, he suffered a devastating knee injury that cost him a full ride to San Jose State and ended his hopes of joining the Giants fraternity.

At that moment, Chet Russell ducked his head in the door and rescued Bernie from reliving the moment he blew out his knee.

"Hey, Commish, did you get my message? The guys have been talking. We need an even *bigger* event this year for the draft. Something that'll be local *and* beat our Vegas trip."

"Yeah, you and everyone else. Listen, can we talk about it a little later? I still need to finish preparing for my meeting with Harbison International, and I'm behind schedule."

"No problem, Bernie. I'll catch up with you later."

When Bernie came back from his meeting, Chet had his feet propped up on Bernie's desk and was sinking Nerf ball after Nerf ball into the little plastic rim and net in the corner of Bernie's tiny office. He was demonstrating the skill he had once displayed as a star point-guard at St. Johns, the all-boys Catholic high school he attended in the small, blue-collar town north of Pittsburgh where he grew up.

"So, as I was saying, Commish, the guys have some stellar ideas for the draft. Lemme trot 'em out for you so you can *visualize* it."

Bernie set his huge stack of work papers on the corner of his desk and resigned himself to sitting through Chet's presentation. He knew better than to stop Chet when he got on a roll. Bernie also knew that Chet liked to do things "big," having grown up in an Italian family where every event was a large to-do, so he prepared himself for some grandiose plan.

With an opening volley of Italian hand gestures, Chet grabbed a black marker and got up to use the white board on Bernie's wall. He printed the word "DRAFT" in smallish letters in the top left portion of the board.

"Bernie, this is last year's draft. It was really cool, but all the travel time cut into our fun. Not only that, but we have better golf courses right in our own backyard. We also have the fabulous Del Mar Racetrack, and we have the famous San Diego weather. Got it?"

"Got it, Chet."

Chet drew an extra large "DRAFT" and circled it in the bottom right portion of the board.

"Now, this is more attuned to the scale I'm thinking about. Think BIG, befitting our name, BIGFFL!!"

"Okay, Chet, tell me more. How BIG?"

"I'm coming to that."

His excitement growing, Chet took a red marker and wrote the words "LINKS" in the bottom left of the board, circling it with a flourish. He took a green marker and wrote the word "PONIES" in the bottom middle of the board, connecting it to the "LINKS" circle with an arrow from left to right. He then connected the "PONIES" circle with the "DRAFT" circle. To round out the diagram, he wrote "BOOZE" above each circle in orange marker.

Completing his diagram, Chet turned around, a huge grin on his face. "Any questions?"

The Commish scratched his chin, pondering the board.

"Well, Bernie?"

"I'm thinking. I'm thinking. Yes, I like it very much. Let's talk details. Have you thought about the golf course?"

"Of course I have. We narrowed it down to Coronado or Torrey Pines. I thought about some of the country clubs, but with our crew, I think we'd be safer at a muni course."

"Yeah, I agree. They'd be more *understanding* of our free spirited approach to the game."

"Right. Now, out of Coronado or Torrey, we like Torrey best, because it's close to the track, and we can catch the first race if we get an early enough set of tee times."

"Agreed. Torrey it is."

"Now, the track part is easy. We just mosey on up after our round."

"What about the draft. Where and when?"

"Easy. We get a suite at the Del Mar Hilton. It's walking distance from the track."

"Transportation?"

"Junk has a buddy who owns a limo service. He'll give us a deal if we use him for the whole day."

"Done. I'll take it from here. We'll let everyone know so they can plan accordingly."

"Oh, and we came up with a name for this. How about the Perfect Day?"

"The Perfect Day? I like it!"

The morning of the first annual official Perfect Day arrived. It was a Friday with a warm, blue sky and a refreshing offshore breeze. To kick off the morning, everyone decided to have breakfast at Sheldon's, a popular dive in Pacific Beach.

Alcazar's Limousine Service made the rounds, collecting everyone. A huge Italian man named Salvatore drove the limo. His chest resembled a large wine barrel and his arms were the size of tree trunks. He had a deep, booming voice and spoke with a heavy Italian accent.

At 6 AM, he picked up Buckeye Bob, who lived at the Village Terrace in a tiny studio apartment. Sal signaled his arrival by thumping the door with his fist. The next-door neighbor, a seventyish, snooping wisp of a woman named Eleanor, peeked out her door. Sal gave her a menacing stare, and she retreated back into her apartment.

Behind Bob's door, Sal heard the jostling of golf clubs and the door knob turning. Emerging from his cave-like condo, Bob looked like a werewolf who would be at home in the woods, looking for his next victim. His hair pointed up at odd angles, his eyes bulged redder than a thermometer, and he smelled of cheap whisky. Glancing past Bob's shoulder, Sal saw the litter of empty bottles and cans, as well as rolling papers and pot residue on a beat-up, old coffee table. Bob had no other furniture except a couple of folding chairs and a small black-and-white TV set with rabbit ears sitting on a bright red Igloo ice chest.

Bob had donned his usual bright orange polo shirt, OP shorts better suited to the beach than the golf course, and thongs. With his clubs draped over his left shoulder, he lost his balance, sagging against the door frame and steadying himself. In his left hand, he held a black thermos bottle, which he handed to Sal.

"I'm Salvatore, but you can call me Sal."

"I'm Bob DiGiorgio, but you can call me Buckeye Bob."

Sal raised the thermos, cold to the touch, and pointed to it. "You want to warm up this coffee before we go? We got a little time."

"Oh, that's not coffee. It's margaritas."

"Okay then. Shall I grab your clubs?"

"Please. I'll take the thermos. I need a drink."

Sal made the rounds, picking up the rest of the crew. Junkyard Dog sported a genuine Cohiba cigar in full flame. The crack-smoking FBI members' contingent of Chet Russell and Pat Rollins, Chet's recent addition as co-owner, argued back and forth about their draft strategy. Ladies' Man left behind a beautiful twenty-one-year-old woman, one of his many "nieces."

As they drove away from the Ladies' Man's house, Chet poked him in the ribs and joked, "Is that your latest, Robert?"

"Nah, just someone I met last night at the Old Ox. She came up to me at the bar and said she had a thing for older, distinguished-looking gentlemen. She wanted me to pretend I was her father. I was happy to accommodate her."

"Wow, Ladies' Man, that's sick."

The Ladies' Man thought about it for a moment, and a big Cheshire Cat grin spread across his face. "Yeah, it is, isn't it? Hey, just as long as she's eighteen, she's fair game. And I'm not really her dad. At least as far as I know."

Bob had drained the contents of his thermos and explored the contents of the limo bar.

"Hey, they got everything here! Except Miller Lite. Shit. All they have is Bud. I hate Bud! Now I'm forced to drink the hard stuff. Anyone want anything? I think I'm going to whip up some more margaritas."

Chet just shook his head.

Sal next collected Exacta, who wore a hideous pair of plaid golf pants and a lemon yellow golf shirt; Slowhand, the only one of the group to rival Buckeye Bob's drinking prowess; and Bernie, looking dapper in a coordinated red and black outfit and Pebble Beach golf hat. Slowhand joined Buckeye Bob in surveying the limo bar and poured a vodka, straight up. Sal picked up Marty Tanaka last. Marty had taken the early bird flight in from Tucson. With everyone on board, they headed out to Sheldon's, a Denny-esque restaurant specializing in hearty breakfasts and the spiciest Bloody Mary in town.

After breakfast burritos, scrambled eggs, home fries, and guacamole bacon cheeseburgers, the group made its way to Torrey Pines, a beautiful golf layout on prime property with gorgeous views of the Pacific Ocean and the San Diego coastline. The three foursomes gathered at the first tee of the north course, the easier of the two courses. Non-BIGFFLers rounded out the group, mostly friends and business acquaintances of the league members, including Don Arlen, yet another J&T colleague, Craig Fairweather, an attorney who had worked with the Ladies' Man on some consulting deals, and Barry Newmark, a neighborhood friend of Bernie's who was nicknamed "The Dentist" because getting him to pay for anything was like pulling teeth. Once the group settled down, Bernie addressed the troops.

"Welcome to the first annual Perfect Day. The game is hero/goat. Here are your scorecards and the rules."

The Commish passed out the scorecards. Slowhand turned to Bob. "What the hell is hero/goat?"

"I have no idea. I don't give a damn anyway. I came here to drink."

"Amen to that, brother."

After he had distributed the scorecards, the Commish resumed his speech.

"In addition to the main game, we have four separate side bets that Exacta is keeping track of: a three-way reverse Nassau with a scalable skins feature, you guys must have read about that one in last month's *Golf Digest*, a five dollar long drive, closest to the pin on all four par-threes, and a modified best ball using the Morehead convention to adjust the handicaps. I'll collect ninety-five dollars from each of you, in addition to the green fees and cart. That'll take care of your stake in the bets. Any questions?"

Everyone stared straight ahead in confusion, contemplating the gibberish they had just heard.

"No? Well, we've got a full day of fun ahead of us, so you might want to pace yourselves. Remember, after we get done, Sal will pick us up and take us to the track. I hope you brought some cash to bet on the ponies. Enough said. Let the Perfect Day begin."

Everyone let out a cheer, and the first foursome of Buckeye Bob, Slowhand, Exacta and the Dentist took the tee. Exacta got off the tee medium length and straight. Buckeye Bob duck-hooked his drive into a clump of trees. Slowhand skied one straight up. It landed about fifty yards out. The Dentist hit the longest drive of the foursome, a beautiful high draw that started at the right edge of the bunker on the right side of the fairway and ended up right center of the fairway in perfect shape. The next two foursomes got off the tee without incident. Chet, Pat, Junk, and Don Arlen were followed by Ladies' Man, Marty, Craig Fairweather, and the Commish.

Two topics dominated conversation out on the course: gambling and the upcoming draft. In addition to the crazy and complex set of wagers the Commish had introduced, each foursome had more of their own.

Exacta's foursome needed a full-time staff to keep track of the different games. As Slowhand addressed his ball on the second tee, Exacta interrupted him. "Okay, guys, let's make this a little more interesting. I want to play lone wolf, and we'll tweak it a little to include some Firth of Clyde elements, you know, from the old Scottish wagering system."

Slowhand sighed and walked over to the others, knowing he would not get his tee shot off until Exacta had his say. One of the most inveterate gamblers of the bunch, Exacta loved the ponies so much that he had attended a special school to learn the finer points of betting on the thoroughbreds. He always kept on the alert for new, innovative ways to wager.

"Alright, I know what lone wolf is, but what the fuck is Firth of Clyde."

Buckeye Bob scratched his head, looking confused. "Glad you know what lone wolf is. I don't even know that."

The Dentist begged off, saying that he did not gamble on principle. "I don't want to get hooked or anything."

Lone wolf involved rotating team leaders and team members on every hole, naming all of the golf course features after animals and howling like a wolf before a tee shot if the player decided to "go it alone" against the other three players. Even more arcane than wolf, Firth of Clyde involved the consumption of a shot of single malt scotch and the playing of bagpipes before each player struck his shot.

The Commish and his foursome expanded their gambling menu to include anything to do with the golf outing, football, baseball, hockey, tennis, curling, NASCAR, politics, and when Grandma Smith planned to cash her next Social Security check. The proposals and counterproposals flew from the first tee shot to the last putt.

"I'll take Clemson and six points."

"In the Clemson game, they'll run out of Gatorade by the third quarter."

"The Dolphins' offensive line will be out for drug violations by game four. They'll get the drugs from the Peruvian place kicker."

"The drink cart won't come around again until the fourteenth hole. And it will be out of little Jack Daniels bottles and ham sandwiches."

"There will still be ham sandwiches, but they will only have cheddar. No Swiss."

"The wind will change from six to seven miles per hour between the ninth and tenth holes. We can measure it with this contraption my wife got me from the Hammacher Schlemmer catalog."

And so on and so forth.

Play moved at a crawl, as it usually did at Torrey Pines, so the foursomes discussed draft picks at length, sometimes resulting in heated arguments.

On the tee of the par-three sixth hole, a hole notorious for long delays, all three foursomes waited, admiring the beautiful view of the ocean and La Jolla in the distance. Always the opportunist, Junk took the opportunity to take bets on the top pick in the upcoming BIGFFL draft.

"Five bucks apiece to enter the contest. Exacta, you start it off.

"No way, Junk. I'm not giving anything away to you knuckleheads. You'll use it against me in the draft"

"Suit yourself. Buckeye?"

"I'm going with my man Bernie Kosar, the pride of Ohio."

"You've got to be kidding me. Is that even his real name?"

"No one can make up a name like that."

"Are you serious, Buckeye? That's the second year in a row. And he stunk last year."

"Hell, yes. That's my choice."

"Ooookay. Chet? Pat? Which one is speaking for you?"

Chet stepped up. "I'll take this one. We've got our money on Cunningham."

"Now we're back on track, Chet. Geez, you even picked a starter. Marty?"

"I'm going with Dan the Man."

"Dan Marino it is."

Out of the group, quarterbacks dominated, with two taking Joe Montana, two taking Randall Cunningham, and one each for Kosar and Marino. Exacta refused to disclose his choice, and Junk chose Chip Lohmiller, the kicker for the Redskins, putting his infamous Chaos Theory™ into action and testing its outer limits.

Not everyone attended the second leg of the Perfect Day at the Del Mar Track. Bob and Slowhand went back to draft headquarters, a suite at the Hilton, to recharge their batteries, which was code for emptying the mini bar. Those who went to the track experienced more of the same perfect weather. Pat Rollins and the Commish won big, with Rollins taking a cool $515 and the Commish winning an exacta. As the final race ended, everyone repaired to the limo for the short ride to the hotel.

The draft itself went off without a hitch. Junk continued with his unconventional approach to the draft, picking place kickers with his second and fourth picks, followed by tight ends with his fifth and seventh rounders. His strategy netted him Billy Joe Turnover (Tolliver) as his first string QB, chosen in the sixth round.

Buckeye Bob once again selected Bernie Kosar as his first string QB, satisfying his need for Browns players, and he then proceeded to add the illustrious names of Rozier and Hoard at running back, Toon and Quick at wide receiver, and four tight ends, thus neglecting to pick a defense for week one.

Going into the first week, the Commish appeared to be the class of the league, with a solid core of Montana to Rice and Barry Sanders, followed by Ladies' Man, who nabbed Cunningham, Gary Anderson, and the rock hard Chargers defense, and the crack smoking combo of Chet and Pat, who had Warren Moon, Thurman Thomas at running back, Sterling Sharpe, and the vaunted Giants defense.

As the first Perfect Day came to a close, the BIGFFL owners wished each other good luck, happy in the knowledge that the event had exceeded their wildest expectations. In the end, the Perfect Day had become entrenched in the lexicon of the BIGFFL.

COMMERCIAL BREAK

A lot can change in ten years. The president of the United States can go from an ultra-conservative, old school Republican with a wife who looks like his grandmother to an ultra-liberal, new wave Democrat who can reinvent the definition of sex. Technology can move light years and revolutionize the way we work and live through something called the World Wide Web. A guy named Tiger Woods can irrevocably change the way we think about golf. Pro football dynasties can shift from San Francisco to Denver.

As the twentieth century slowly ground to a close, the Cold War that menaced the world for half a century vanished, soon to be replaced by a new kind of fear. The world struggled with the concept of global warming and a troublesome development called the Y2K bug. The Simpsons and Seinfeld became household names.

Closer to home, our BIGFFL heroes matured, got married, raised families and generally got on with their lives. Buckeye Bob tamed down the drinking and married a dark-haired beauty named Rachel.

The Commish had a couple of boys, mainly to ensure a succession line to the Commish role after he stepped down. Chet likewise had children—two boys and two girls—outdoing the Commish in a friendly rivalry. Exacta, Junk, and Slowhand also started families.

J&T, the core of the BIGFFL world in the early years, fell by the wayside as Ladies' Man finally took his early retirement, and Junk left, soon followed by Chet, Exacta, and the Commish. Each went his separate way, settling into executive management roles with various companies. The new core became the BIGFFL, the place where everyone could stay in touch and get caught up.

Among all of the change, two things stayed the same. Like the swallows coming back to you-know-where, Bob continued to lose, year in and year out. He couldn't kick the Browns habit, no matter how hard he tried.

As the last year of the millennium waned and everyone ran around worrying about Y2K, the Commish made final preparations for the tenth anniversary of the BIGFFL. They were returning to Vegas, where they had not been in nine years. He booked a suite at Caesars Palace similar to the one they had occupied in 1990. The plan was the same as before: two days of gambling, draft, and golf.

The same group made the trek, although Chet, Junk, Exacta, and Slowhand missed the first day of gambling because of various family commitments that included youth soccer, Pop Warner football, dance recitals, and birthday parties. Of the five owners who came in early, the Commish had a last-minute report to get out for work, Ladies' Man took a nap, Marty Tanaka opted to gamble on his own, swearing off his fellow owners as "bad luck," Buckeye Bob spent his time making last-minute preparations for the draft, and Pat Rollins spent the day riding around in a limo trying to pick up women off the street.

As in prior years, the draft began around 7:30 PM. The owners arrived promptly, drinking about 1.5 beers apiece before settling into the dining table.

The Commish surveyed the scene in front of him, shaking his head, and addressed the group.

"Geez. You guys look like a bunch of old men. I think I'll call room service and have them send up a bottle of Geritol. We can do shots before we start the draft. Let's get down to business, I e-mailed you guys the updated rules and the links to the Website. Check out your passwords and make sure they work. I don't want someone calling me on Sunday morning whining about how they can't get in, Marty. There aren't any major rule changes, so there should be no surprises.

"You already have the order of the draft, but just to be safe, it is: Buckeye Bob, Slowhand, Cactus, Exacta, Ladies' Man, Crack Smokers, Junk and the Commish. The always observant Commish wants you to know that some things never change, like our friend Buckeye Bob selecting first by virtue of his last place finish, and the perennial excellence of the Commish, who selects first by virtue of a stellar year where I kicked all of your asses up one side and down the other. Aficionados of history will note that was my second crown, tying Ladies' Man for the most in our league history.

"One other item. We are inaugurating a new trophy this year, the Bernard I. Gregory Fantasy Football League trophy. Bowing to your overwhelming protest, I scrapped the idea for a replica of me on the trophy, so we have a football player with a pseudo-Heisman pose instead. That's about it. Any questions? Of course Marty has a question. What Marty?"

"Hey Commish-in-Error, do you have an off knob somewhere on you? Every year your speeches get longer and longer. I'm glad we have A/C in here with all the hot air blowin' around."

The Commish chuckled and replied, "The only thing that's blowing tonight is you, as soon as you can get out of here and find a guy to your liking. Okay, draft away."

Bob selected quickly. "For the first pick of the 10th annual BIGFFL draft, Buckeye Bob selects Tim Couch, quarterback for the Cleveland Browns."

Everyone knew where Bob was heading again this year. Back to the cellar.

THE SECOND QUARTER

On Independence Day 2004, Bob and his wife Rachel went out to Ski Beach, as they did every year, to watch the fireworks. The skies pulsated with brilliant pyrotechnics. Bob held Rachel close as they looked up together, enjoying the beauty and the power of the display. After the explosions subsided, relative quiet—interspersed with rumblings of people packing up their chairs, sports gear, and ice chests—punctuated the night.

Knowing the traffic would take at least an hour to clear out, Bob and Rachel usually took a walk in the sand along the water, unwinding, talking about nothing in particular. This year Bob did all the talking.

"Rach, I think I have this BIGFFL thing figured out. All those years of failures are going to end this year. I'm going to win it all."

For a moment, Rachel drew a blank. They had not spoken of the BIGFFL since last January, when another dismal failure of a season had ended, making it a string of fourteen losing seasons in a row. It took her a moment to tune in. The BIGFFL? In July? Bob had always been enthusiastic about his fantasy football, but never this fanatical. Confused, she remained silent and continued to listen to his rant.

"You see, there are a couple of tricks that make the difference. The Defense. Big D. Defense. And the backup quarterback. Gotta have that. Oh, and the receivers. Those receivers are critical. Not to mention running backs. Gotta have good running backs. Throw it all together and mix it in. And the draft prep. Gotta have everything at my fingertips. All on the laptop so I can run scenarios. That's the real secret. Scenarios. That's the gold mine."

Bob's eyes, tinged red, looked like something out of *Rosemary's Baby* as he continued to lay out his newfound wisdom to Rachel.

"I've been focused on ESPN a lot lately. The camps are in full swing now. The machinery is in motion. Decisions are being made. The inevitable is unfolding. We've got new coaches, lots of exciting trades, and some fabulous draft picks. It's really going to complicate things. This gives smart guys like me an advantage. Just think. I could pick Terrell Owens. He might be my number one. He's with the high-powered Eagles now, with McNabb. That's all that was missing for them to win a Super Bowl. T.O. He's the key to everything. Or maybe he's not my first pick, but my second? Gotta play it cool. You see, I pick first, which is great, but it also means I need to make that first pick count, because I don't get another shot until pick sixteen. But the biggest key of all, I have to stay away from the Brownies. They're just no good for me. It's gonna be tough, but I think I finally have it licked. If I can do that, I'm gonna have me a winner!"

At 8 AM, Bob usually left for work, but on July fifth, when Rachel looked in on him before leaving for work, she found him in the home

office glued to the computer, dressed in a pair of sweats and a ratty old Over the Line T-shirt.

"What's going on, Bob? Are you going in late today?"

"No, I'm taking the day off. I need to spend the day laying out my draft strategy. One day off won't hurt. My staff has everything under control."

"Okay, if you say so."

Rachel said nothing as she left. Baxter, a ten-year-old golden retriever, sidled up to Bob and lay down next to him, pleased that he had some human companionship instead of an empty house. Oblivious, Bob surfed the web, hitting all of the fantasy football sites, gleaning information, and entering it into his custom database.

"Shit. I need more data. The web doesn't have enough to make my 3-D draft model really HUM!"

Bob jumped in his Lexus and drove to Borders. He began yanking fantasy football publications from the shelves, piling them into a wire shopping basket. For a brief moment, he got sidetracked investigating the credentials of Dory, the *Penthouse* Pet for August, but he decided that wouldn't help him with the draft and, with great difficulty, set it aside.

As he made his way to the checkout counter, he took a detour to the music section, slapping on some headphones to listen to the Ohio State fight songs "Buckeye Battle Cry" and "Across the Field" and blasting some Van Halen, which he had been craving for quite some time.

When he checked out, Estelle the cashier rang up his purchases.

"Sir, with your Borders discount, that will be $215.36. You also get a complimentary Lindt truffle of your choice."

"Huh, ain't that somethin'?"

"Yes, it is, sir."

Bob fumbled in his pocket, pulled out a dog-eared black wallet chock full of various pieces of paper and cards, sorted through scraps advertising fantasy football league hotlines and cheat sheets, and eventually produced a Platinum American Express card.

"Put it on this, Estelle."

After signing the credit card receipt, Bob hefted his large bags of magazines and made his way to the car, content that he now had sufficient information to build a foolproof database, one that would produce 99.9 percent reliable information and allow him to run any "what if" modeling scenario and binomial calculations he required.

"Too bad I don't have enough cash for a Cray supercomputer. That would really put me over the top. Rent a flatbed and bring it with me to the draft. Boy, the Commish would shit if he saw that. I'm done being a loser. Bob's not going to be anyone's doormat anymore."

August 2004 arrived. The baseball season dragged to a conclusion. Fantasy baseball began to wear on its participants, as it always did when the real deal—fantasy football—neared.

Ladies' Man, the Commish of the fantasy baseball league (FBL), put in his time, waiting it out. About to be eliminated from any chance at the championship, his interest waned. Chet Russell had already been eliminated. They couldn't wait until the FBL ended.

One day, Chet got on the phone to the Commish.

"Hey, Commish. I'm tired of this roundball shit. When's the Perfect Day? And what's the draft order?"

"Damn, Chet. Don't you read your e-mail? It's August thirty-first. My staff has lined up the venue, the cuisine is ready to go, and draft headquarters is prepared and waiting. The draft order is Buckeye Bob,

Slowhand, Exacta, Cactus Connection, Junkyard Dog, Ladies' Man, you, and me. I've got an e-mail coming out shortly."

"Thanks- Commish. Hey, we should hook up for lunch and discuss draft strategy. And by the way, you mentioned the golf, food, and draft. What about the women?"

"Those days are long gone, Chet. Nice try."

For the past ten years, with the exception of the tenth anniversary return to Vegas, the Perfect Day had been held at Singing (aka, Singeing) Hills Golf Course. The Commish liked this venue because of its proximity to his East County mansion—even though it approximated hell, with ninety-five degrees of 100 percent humidity heat.

The latest installment of the Perfect Day golf outing boasted a larger group of players than the first version. There were six foursomes in all, as the inaugural group of golfers had been joined by friends from fantasy baseball and others from their various circles. The trip to the race track had long since become a casualty of the group's busy schedule, compounded by the logistics of trying to play golf in El Cajon, get out to the coast for the races, and come back to El Cajon for the draft.

Each man had his ritual. Buckeye Bob and Slowhand had bonded early in the league and started going to Perry's Diner after Sheldon's shut down. The legendary Perry's, housed in an old Sambo's restaurant, boasted a large cross section of diners from San Diego's Who's Who list. Signed photos on the walls attested to this fact.

When Slowhand arrived at 9 AM, their usual time, Buckeye Bob gave him an enthusiastic welcome.

"Well, Bob, another season, huh?"

"Yeah. Most importantly, I can't wait for the food. I love this place."

They made for the front counter, where the owner's wife, Gwen, took their name.

"Five minutes, guys."

"That's not bad. So are you ready for the draft, Slowhand?"

"I haven't done shit yet. I think I'm gonna wing it. I get the same result no matter what I do anyway. How about you, Bob?"

"I got a system this year. A very sophisticated algorithm that predicts all possible combinations and rates them according to the Kleinschmidt rule of probable outcomes. It has Chaos Theory™ beat by a mile."

"Wow, sounds pretty complicated."

"I rented time on a Cray supercomputer to process it. I downloaded the program onto my laptop so I can make some final adjustments."

Slowhand noticed that Bob had a black IBM laptop wedged under his arm.

"Clapton, party of two."

"That's us, Bob."

The waitress, Roz, a veteran who had been at Perry's since Bob and Slowhand started coming here, showed them to a small booth opposite the counter.

"Hi, boys. Long time no see. Coffee?"

"Black."

"Coke for me."

"I know what I'm getting." Slowhand didn't pick up a menu.

"If I remember correctly, chili omelet, side of guac, home fries, and blueberry muffin."

"Got it."

The food came, and the two settled down to the most anticipated meal of their year.

At the golf course, Chet of CSFBIM had already hit the range to work on his hopeless excuse for a golf swing. He had hit two large buckets, his lime green shirt drenched with sweat, and developed a vicious case of the shanks for his trouble.

The Commish, Junk, and Ladies' Man arrived early as well, taking their customary spots in the coffee shop for sandwiches and conversation. They deemed themselves the Rules Committee—a euphemism for bookies—and used the time to construct ever more elaborate gambling schemes.

Slowhand, Bob, and the rest of the group came straggling in about a half hour before their tee times, joined by the traveling element, including Marty Tanaka, fresh from a Southwest flight from Tucson.

Besides Marty, the tournament attracted a number of nonleague travelers, guys like Max Weingard, a hard-drinking, cigar-chomping, barrel-chested, larger-than-life stockbroker from New York. He came in wearing the finest apparel with a cell phone on each ear as he lugged his huge Ping tournament bag and golf shoes.

Phone #1: "Nail that son-of-a-bitch down on the margin trade!"

Phone #2: "You better sell the minute it hits 23 1/8 or I'll kick your ass from here to Albany."

Satisfied until the next call, Max snapped each phone shut and put one in each pocket like a gunfighter holstering his Colt 45s.

No one liked Max, nor did anyone know how such a pompous ass had gotten into the group. The group tolerated him only because of his J&T alumni status. Seeing the Commish at his customary table, Max made a beeline.

"Bernard, how the hell are ya?"

The Commish nodded. "Max."

"Did I tell you how much I made last week? I bought another string of ponies just on one day's commissions."

"That so, Max? Well, that's just fabulous."

"Well, I'm off for my single malt, Cohiba, and warm-up session."

"Hit 'em straight," mumbled the Commish, hoping Max would have a miserable round.

A number of other long-distance travelers had been coming for years. Marlon Rivers had a great disposition and everyone liked him. Another J&T alum, he now owned a string of used car lots in Omaha, Nebraska. Ferrell McGee practiced as an attorney and had represented J&T in various litigation matters. He had retired some years ago and bought a villa in Baja California, making this one of his few trips out of Mexico.

After the session on the range, most of the players gathered on the putting green to get caught up, as many had not seen each other since the end of the last football season.

"Buckeye Bob. How the hell are ya? How's Rachel doing?"

"Great, Junk, how goes it with you? How's the kid's golf game?"

"Never better, Bob. He won four out of five junior tournaments he played over the past four months, and he qualified for the US Amateur."

"Congratulations! Helluva kid, that Jason!"

Over on the edge of the practice green, Marty Tanaka, Chet, Exacta, and Slowhand huddled together. Chet regaled the group with tales of his summer vacation.

"Man, that fish was fighting so hard. It took me four hours to bring him in. The boys helped me the whole way. They threw water on the reel to keep it cool, brought me beers, and generally hung in. And the girls helped their mother cook the monster after we landed it! That was a great trip, I tell ya."

Marty chuckled.

"Sounds like a hot time there, Chet."

"It was, Marty. Why? What did you do this summer?"

"Well, I'll tell ya Chet. I got laid as much as possible. You know, Lake Havasu is just crawling with women during the summer. I just go out there and hang out the open for business sign."

Exacta rolled his eyes.

"Like the babes at Havasu are gonna get within a hundred feet of an ugly bastard like you."

"Yeah, well what did you do this summer, Exacta? Attend Gamblers Anonymous meetings?"

"That's pretty funny for a fuckwit like you, Marty. Actually, my wife and I went to Kauai and relaxed. Hung out at the pool, the beach. Literally did nothing. And check this out. The missus and I are grandparents. Can you believe it? Grandparents!"

Chet pretended to size Exacta up. "Way to go, Perry. I can't believe you're a grandfather. No, wait a minute. On second thought, you look older than dirt, man. I'm surprised you're not a *great* grandfather by now."

As everyone laughed, the Commish reappeared from his "office" in the coffee shop with a bullhorn.

"Okay BIGFFLers and friends. Welcome to the fourteenth annual Perfect Day. This day has been preceded by the most elaborate planning to date. I think you will all be impressed. The game is the same, hero/goat. At great expense, I have personally printed the scorecards that you will find in your carts. For those of you who are math-challenged, I have removed the idiot factor. That is, all you have to do is write your score in the appropriate boxes. I will do the rest. And remember, I will not listen to any of your bitching!!"

The crowd booed and hissed.

41

"You all have your tee times. Ladies' Man, the sergeant-at-arms, will collect the greens fee, as well as the ten dollar mulligan fee, a new tradition that will entitle you to one mulligan per nine. Use it at your discretion, but use it wisely. Other than that, gentlemen, start your engines, and may the best man win."

Just as the group turned to the tee to watch the first group, Chet's partner Pat came running in, out of breath. A high-powered software engineer for Techcom, the technology giant, Pat always seemed to be flying in from some exotic locale, this time from Bali.

On the first tee, the players faced the toughest shot of the day, not because of the hole itself, an easy par four, but because all eyes watched every move and woe to anyone who didn't hit a good shot, took too long to hit the ball, or didn't look good doing it.

The first group contained Chet, Pat, Slowhand, and Max the stockbroker. Marty Tanaka always requested the last group just so he could heckle all the groups before him, forgetting that heckling could be just as bad on the eighteenth, where everyone gathered round the green to trash even the slightest imperfection in a shot. He had taken up his perch just to the left of the tee. Junk also had a reputation as a famous heckler. He analyzed each swing according to its consistency with the tenets of the Chaos Theory™.

Max, who had shaved his head between last year and this year, played first. He took a big drag of his Cohiba, tossed it aside, and swaggered up to his ball with his driver, a club that had been made for him by a ninety-year-old master club maker from the Duff House Golf Club in the old country of Banff, Scotland.

"Hey, Max, nice haircut."

"Thanks, Marty."

Max proceeded to power push his shot into the deep gorge fronting the tee.

"Nice drive, Max. You got all of that one."

Max slammed his thousand-dollar driver into the ground, almost snapping the shaft in two.

Slowhand took the tee box next. He always tended to wear bright clothing, usually in neon orange or lime green. This year, he had a Rorschach inkblot shirt on, enough to make anyone within one hundred yards get vertigo.

"Hey, Slowhand, who puked on your shirt?"

"Geez, Slowhand, why don't you wear something that doesn't make everyone dizzy next time?"

Ignoring the gallery, Slowhand stepped up and smacked his drive 280 yards down the right center of the fairway, in perfect position. Good shots always had a habit of silencing the critics, as did this one.

Chet pulled out his trusty Callaway Great Big Bertha, teed up a Top Flite and went through his preshot routine, standing behind the ball, surveying the fairway, stepping up, waggling the club head three times, and sending out his usual 220-yard fade down the center of the fairway. He turned around and bowed to the mock applause.

Pat teed off last. Despite his wealth, Pat still played with a genuine wood driver, circa 1974. With a jerky swing reminiscent of Ray Floyd on crystal meth, Pat hit a bizarre tee shot—the ball hooked left, deflected off a large oak, and came to rest in the bunker left of the landing area.

The festivities had begun.

After about five hours of wicked heat and questionable golf, the groups meandered around the eighteenth green, grabbing any available shade from the surrounding oaks, their carts parked too close to the green.

Of the six foursomes, all but one—Commish, Marty Tanaka, Exacta, and Marlon Rivers—had already finished. While they waited for the last foursome, a hole and a half behind, three players practiced putts on the green. The rest spoke about the coming football season, business, family, and whatever else came to mind. They had also placed additional side bets on who in the final foursome would shoot the best score on the eighteenth, a short par three with a two-tier green surrounded by bunkers, requiring anywhere from a six iron to a nine iron, depending on the player and the wind.

Slowhand: "Okay, I'm taking the Commish on this one. He's been on all day."

Junk: "On what? Prozac? Valium? Rogaine?"

Chet: "I'll take Exacta. I think he can nail it with his seven metal. He's got that thing wired."

Junk: "It definitely won't be Tanaka. He's so muscled up he'll either air mail it into the river bed behind the green or miss it entirely. The fact that he has no neck is a severe disadvantage. I'll take Marlon. He may not get it closest on his approach, but he'll prevail with his used car salesman finesse around the green."

Brandishing his Ping Eye II seven iron, the Commish tossed up some grass to check the direction of the wind and stepped up to his ball. After a couple of waggles, he launched it straight and true, nestling it ten feet to the right of the pin, which sat on the green's upper tier. Raucous applause greeted the shot.

"Way to go, Commish."

"Helluva shot."

"You suck."

"Nicely done, girly-man."

Marty stepped up next, a pitching wedge in hand. With a mighty backswing, the shaft of the club straining, his club way past parallel at the top, Marty came back through, taking a massive divot and missing the ball, which remained on the tee. The divot flew about forty yards.

"Got all a that one, Marty."

Sheepish, Marty looked around and muttered, "Practice swing." Murmurs of "bullshit" greeted him from the others in the foursome. Collecting himself, Marty ramped up to a nine iron, plunking his second shot into the front right bunker. The ball disappeared under the sand, ensuring him a difficult third shot to the green.

Exacta executed an efficient seven-metal to just below the upper tier, leaving a tricky side-hill, two-break putt. Marlon sculled an eight iron that skipped from the front of the green, bypassed the pin, and settled on the first cut of fringe on the back of the green, fifteen feet behind the pin. It was a great result for a poor effort.

As the foursome approached the green, they placed additional bets on Marty, such as how many shots it would take him to escape the bunker, his final score, and how many clubs he would throw in anger.

Marty lumbered into the trap, addressed the spot where he thought his ball lay, and took another prodigious swing. The ball remained buried, though he could now see it. His face growing beefsteak tomato red, he took another big pass, this time moving the ball about eighteen inches, now unburied. In frustration, he swung again with the same intensity, sending the ball over the green and into the river bed. He turned and snapped the lob wedge over his knee, which brought a mix of wild cheering and catcalls from the gallery, then strode to the cart, popped open a Sam Adams, and contemplated additional club alteration.

"Put me down for a ten."

As it turned out, Marlon lipped out a very good chip, settling for a par, Exacta three-putted for a bogey four, and the Commish sunk his ten-footer for a birdie. As they settled bets, the drink cart, absent for the majority of the round, motored around the corner, trying to speed past the group and make a getaway. Ladies' Man threw himself in front of the cart, stopping it. The driver, a twenty-something blonde with headlights larger than a bus, plus a great figure and a short skirt, popped out of the cart, surprised at Ladies' Man's intervention.

"Hello, darlin'. Think I could get something cold to fight the heat?"

Ladies' Man approached the girl, then turned toward his fellow BIGFFLers and shouted, "Hey guys, you want anything?"

A dozen tired, thirsty, and horny men rushed the unfortunate girl. By the time she had filled the orders, she had sold an assortment of beers, cigars, Gatorades, small bottles of rum and vodka, Snickers and Three Musketeers bars, bottled waters, and Diet Cokes. Her tip made it all worthwhile, and she lit up with a smile as she plopped back in her seat and drove off.

Drinks in hand, the guys milled around the back of the green like cattle, debating the finer points of draft strategy and anticipating the big event about to take place.

Exacta kicked off the discussion, looking up from his racing form. "The key is to pick up the best QB right away. They're always guaranteed to score the most points. You get a good one, he'll anchor your season."

Marty shook his head. "Give me a running back like Priest Holmes, a machine. That's what I want."

Slowhand lamented, "I always get burned on the defenses. I have a solid lineup, then I get stuck with some defense like the Browns that gives me negative thirty points and I give it all back."

Chet and Pat, joined at the hip, contributed their wisdom in unison like a bizarre mutation of Tweedle Dum and Tweedle Dee. "It's critical to have a solid system, not just to focus on positions. We have a sophisticated model we use. We call it the crack-o-meter. Just look at our record to see how successful it's been."

"Screw that. You guys are the luckiest assholes in the world. My approach is to keep the details out of it. I go by the seat of my pants. No use cluttering up my head with useless things like facts." Marty began to get agitated, prompting Junk to join the conversation.

"That explains your past success, Marty." Everyone chuckled. "Listen, you guys all know that proper application of the Chaos Theory™ is the only way to go. I proved it already, and I stand by my conclusions."

Pat, venturing out on his own without Chet, said, "You mean the one where you draft kickers in the first four rounds and tight ends in the next three? Yeah, right. That's worked real well for you, Junk. Whaddaya have, one championship and a string of second division finishes? Sounds like the Chaos Theory™ ain't all it's cracked up to be."

"That's only because we're not on a level playing field in the BIGFFL. We don't have a pure environment to effectively test the underlying assumptions. Unfortunately, the Commish has queered the experiment."

Exacta came to the Commish's rescue, who was in the clubhouse tallying up the scores. "Hey, that's not fair, Junk. The Commish isn't here to defend himself. The only queer in the group is you."

"Yeah, whatever. I'm getting another Bushmills. Anyone else want anything?"

Junk had been a proponent of the Chaos Theory™ since he had discovered it during his undergraduate computer science days at Arizona State. He used the theory in all aspects of his life, including his fantasy football draft strategy. Ever since the inaugural BIGFFL season, the success of the Chaos Theory™ had been a source of friendly debate and contention among the league members, prompting sometimes passionate argument from the Junk camp.

When Junk returned to the table, Bushmills in hand, he appeared ready to renew the longstanding debate.

"You guys just don't understand the Chaos Theory™. Let me try to explain it to you one more time. You see, the Chaos Theory™ is founded in random mathematics, and one of the major premises is that small inputs can have big outputs. For example, a butterfly flapping its wings in Africa in 1945 can cause a tornado in Kansas forty-seven years later. Or, a person flapping their jaw and releasing hot air in El Cajon for three years can cause a hurricane in Florida. Or, a Charger fan watching a satellite transmission in Florida can cure a ten-year playoff drought.

"All of these random, Chaotic Event Chains™ cross our lives every day, and it is up to the individual to receive the 'vibes' and manage their lives. However, the mind is not capable of always sorting out all the numerous complex chains. Hence we have what are commonly known as 'mistakes.' By definition, 'mistakes' are only known after the fact, whereas Chaotic Chain Watching™ and Pattern Recognition™ are predictors. Whether you package it as 'vibes,' 'intuition,' 'sixth sense,' or whatever, it's all the same skill.

"The Junkyard Dogs have one of the better three-year records in the league. Chaotic Chain Watching™ has gotten me there, and it will keep me there. Now do you get it?"

Those who had been stupid enough to listen to Junk's speech stood around speechless, mouths agape, catching flies and trying to figure out what the hell this had to do with fantasy football. Oblivious, Junk stalked off to get yet another Bushmills, satisfied that he had educated the masses.

While everyone else drank, smoked, and defended their draft strategies around the eighteenth green, Buckeye Bob sat in his cart, oblivious to it all. He had his laptop and stacks of binders and papers spread across the seat, appraising them, shaking his head, and talking to himself.

Buckeye Bob oozed confidence because he felt he had perfected his computer model and calculated 99.9 percent of the possibilities and permutations that would lead him to a winning season. He now struggled with a qualitative issue much more difficult to tackle because it could not be reduced to formulas and calculations—his loyalty to his home team, the hapless Cleveland Browns. He always picked Browns, and it always came back to haunt him. This year, he had altered his strategy, facing reality and putting a limitation on how many Browns he would select. Now he just had to decide where to make the cut. This made him very anxious.

While Bob puzzled out this dilemma, Ladies' Man approached him, slapping him on the back and blowing cigar smoke in his face.

"Yo, Bob. What's happenin'? Got it all figured out?"

"Hey, Ladies' Man. Yeah, I think this is my year. I feel pretty good about it."

"You don't say? So share your secret with me."

"There's no real secret. Just good old-fashioned elbow grease and a very sophisticated computer program."

The Ladies' Man raised his eyebrow and shook his head, remembering thirteen seasons ago when he had encountered Bob in a very similar scene. Back then, Bob had several publications spread out and pages of green ledger paper with notations of statistics and probabilities. Now he had the laptop and computer printouts. Despite the passage of years, the look on his face remained the same, a mix of zeal and enthusiasm as he pursued his quest for that elusive combination that would produce a winning season. A small grin came across the L-Man's face. Some things never change.

"Ah, I see. Well, good luck my man. See you at the Commish's house."

"Okay, listen up guys," the Commish shouted, back from the clubhouse. "Let's all gather round the back of the green for the annual BIGFFL commemorative photo. Arrange yourselves in three rows, like we did last year. Now if we can just find someone to take the picture."

No one except the BIGFFL group stood around the eighteenth tee or on the nearby seventeenth fairway. The Commish began to get in his cart to ask someone from the clubhouse to come out and take the picture, when the erstwhile cart girl reappeared. She tried to pretend she didn't see the Commish waving her down, but once again Ladies' Man stood between the girl and her escape route.

"Not so fast, sweetheart. We need a little help. If you'd be so kind as to take our picture, why we shore would appreciate it."

She got out of the cart and, with a bashful smile, accepted the camera from Ladies' Man, readying herself to take the picture as the group moved into place.

"Is everyone ready? On a count of three. One, two, three."

The picture came out perfect. Everyone had a big smile, especially Buckeye Bob, who dominated the center of the picture with a confident grin and a double thumbs-up.

Once the golf match ended, the group made a mad dash to the Commish's house for the final installment of the Perfect Day: the draft.

The group usually caravanned to the Commish's house about a mile away. The Commish lived in an exclusive gated community, Besa Cola, and as seemed to happen every year, everyone always forgot the password to the gate. Sure enough, when the Commish arrived at the gate after tallying the scores in the golf course bar, he saw the now-familiar line of cars out to the street, all waiting to get in.

"What the hell is the password again?"

The Commish punched in the three-digit code, and everyone negotiated the gate.

They wound through a neighborhood of beautiful custom-built homes, each on an acre or more of land. The Commish himself had a home perched atop a hill, his backyard overlooking the fourth hole. When the league started, the Commish's house stood alone, surrounded by vacant lots. Now neighbors encroached on every side.

As league members arrived, they went through the side gate to the backyard, taking up positions on the patio furniture or at the card tables set up for the draft. As they waited for the pizza to arrive, they grabbed cold beverages and observed another annual ritual.

The Commish came around back with a plastic bag full of balls his kids retrieved from the golf course lakes. He poured the bag out onto his immaculate back lawn. All of the others wandered over with drivers in their hands.

Each person took their best shot at the fourth green, some 280 yards below. To make the shot even tougher, a large lake fronted the narrow two-tiered green. The winner won the pot, which was two bucks a shot from each participant.

Player after player took their best shot. Without exception, every ball found its way back into its watery grave, with the exception of Junk and Max, who found the bottom tier of the green furthest from the pin, positioned near the back of the top tier. Buckeye Bob ambled up to the makeshift teeing ground next. He stood over the ball with intense concentration. After what seemed an hour, he began his slow takeaway. Anyone close to him would have heard him hum "Blue Danube," a trick to keep his tempo slow. At the top, he continued past parallel, the shaft bowing far past parallel. He let the club come back through, catching the ball right on the screws. No one doubted the outcome. The ball soared and landed on the front tier, rolling up onto the top tier and coming to rest about ten feet from the pin.

The group let out a big yell and each man took his turn congratulating Buckeye Bob on an excellent shot.

"Here you go, Bob. Eighty-four dollars. That'll pay for most of your league dues anyway."

"Thanks, Commish," Bob beamed.

In what couldn't have been better timing, the Gregory family's hot babysitter Gail arrived with an armful of pizza boxes. Ladies' Man greeted the barely legal young lady with a peck on each cheek. The glorious smells of fresh sausage, pepperoni, tomato sauce, and garlic permeated the air, summoning the famished participants and creating a literal run for the kitchen. Having bought pizzas for last year's draft as well, Gail learned her lesson. She dropped the pizzas on the counter and made herself scarce as the group pried open pizza boxes and each man took two or three large slices at a time. The pieces oozed cheese and emitted steam. While everyone else swarmed the pizza, Ladies' Man slipped away, following Gail to the back room.

Near-silence ensued for the next fifteen minutes as everyone ate. Afterward, each team owner took up a position on the patio. Buckeye Bob took a generous amount of space, setting up his laptop and arraying a series of binders to his right. Junk had also brought a laptop and a formidable chunk of information, which he spread out around him. Both fussed over their mathematical theories, fine-tuning and tweaking to the last minute.

Others, not as prepared, rushed to get ready in states ranging from nonchalant to panicked as they realized they didn't have a clue who to select. The Commish planned to rely on his son Lucas. Chet and Pat of CSFBIM engaged in their perennial discussion regarding who had been responsible for researching and setting strategy.

"Pat, I told you to go out and buy the magazines. You were going to set up the grid for us."

"No way, Chet. I thought you were going to do it. You do it every year anyway. You never let me make any real decisions."

Exacta and Slowhand each had a couple of the popular fantasy football magazines and cheat sheets. Marty Tanaka had a single piece of paper he had ripped out of one of the magazines, featuring a picture of a partially disrobed cheerleader. When asked his strategy, he replied, "I'm going with my instincts."

The Commish stood to address the group.

"Okay. We're going to start in a couple of minutes. Is everyone here?"

Everyone looked around.

"I think we're missing Ladies' Man."

At that moment, Ladies' Man strode onto the back patio, bright red lipstick on his collar and a shit-eating grin on his face.

"Thanks for defiling my babysitter, Ladies' Man. Tell you what, good babysitters are hard to find, so next time you get within ten paces of her, you get a ten dollar fine."

"Well worth it, my man. Well worth it."

"How many Cialis capsules did you have to pop for that five minutes of happiness, old man?" Marty Tanaka sneered.

"No foreign agents involved, Cactus. All natural talent."

As everyone finished their preparation, Ladies' Man strode around the backyard like a peacock, gleaning any bits of knowledge from the teams he could overhear. Teams shielded their precious draft wisdom from him as he approached. To his benefit, Ladies' Man possessed a sixth sense that enabled him to excel year after year. He absorbed information by osmosis as he read the sports page to get information on the daily horse races. He and everyone else knew he was ready.

"Okay, gents, and I use that term VERY loosely, you know the order of the draft. The first pick of the fifteenth annual BIGFFL draft goes to Buckeye Bob DiGiorgio. Bob?"

Bob executed a couple of keystrokes on his laptop, waited for the CPU to process his adjustments, and broke out in a big grin.

"For the first pick of the fifteenth annual BIGFFL draft, the Buckeye Bobs take Attoi Roi."

Around the table, the silence was deafening. Then the questions kicked in.

"Huh? Who the hell is that?

"How do you spell it?"

"What position does he play?"

"What team is he with?"

"I think I knew a Follies Bergere dancer in Paris with that name. Did she take up football?"

"It's spelled A-T-T-O-I R-O-I. R-O-I, as in return on investment. He's not a Follies Bergere dancer. He's the new quarterback for the high-powered New Orleans Saints, and my computer program says he will score 453 points for me this year. If he even comes close, I've got it made."

While everyone else questioned Bob's pick, Ladies' Man reviewed his notes. When the noise died down, he resettled his glasses on his nose and nodded toward Bob.

"That's a helluva pick, Buckeye. My research notes say Roi is a phenomenal talent out of the Big Easy, a three-sport player out of high school: baseball, basketball, and football. He's stepping in for the injured Aaron Brooks, who's out for the season. In fact, I had him pegged for my third or fourth round pick if he was still around because he tore it up during the preseason. Nicely done."

Slowhand came next. He selected Peyton Manning.

Marty steamed, "Damn! That was going to be my pick."

When Exacta's turn came, he meandered over his papers as minutes passed.

Ladies' Man prompted, "Hey, Exacta, while we're still young."

Marty did a slow boil, bothered by the long wait. "Tell you what, Exacta. I'm going to go eat three pieces of pizza, have two beers, have sex with the first hot chick I see, and play eighteen holes. I should be back just in time to make my pick."

CSFBIM hummed the theme to *Jeopardy* in unison.

Exacta ignored these taunts as he continued to pore through his papers. When he had completed his deliberations, he cleared his throat.

"For the third pick of the fifteenth annual BIGFFL draft, Exacta selects Marshall Faulk."

Ladies' Man reacted to this dubious selection first. "Great pick, Exacta. I heard he'll only be out for about five games this year."

Tanaka scowled. "We waited twenty-three minutes for that Einstein move? The good news is we don't have to worry too much about Exacta's team, at least on the strength of that pick."

The Commish, munching a slice of pizza with the works—including anchovies—now weighed in with one of his typical edicts.

"In keeping with the tradition of the great Kennesaw Mountain Landis, former commissioner and resident fascist of Major League

Baseball, I hereby decree that no team shall take more than one minute to select his draft pick going forward. The sergeant at arms will closely monitor this and violators will never play professional baseball again."

Marty banged the table.

"Excellent! Now let's get on with it. I take Culpepper for my first pick. Your turn, Junk."

"After carefully applying the Chaos Theory™ in the form of the chaotic draft model, version 3.1, the Junkyard Dogs select Antonio Gates as their first pick."

"There's a good choice, Junk. I'd take eight to ten points a game any day over the fourteen to eighteen points a game that McNabb, Tomlinson, or Alexander would give me."

"You don't understand the Chaos Theory™, Marty. You never have, and you never will."

"Maybe not, but I usually like to select players with a good chance of getting me more points instead of less. That's according to the Marty theory of severe ass kicking."

"You're up, Ladies' Man."

"Well, you guys have kind of thrown a wrench into my finely tuned methodology, but you left a few crumbs on the table. I think I'll take Mr. Donovan McNabb, the Campbell's Soup icon. He seems to have a good year ahead of him."

Pat and Chet of CSFBIM battled back and forth without reaching agreement, arguing like an old married couple and jabbing their cheat sheets to emphasize their respective points. After several minutes, they reached an uneasy accord, signified by Chet's shrugging of his shoulders and heavy sigh.

"Can I at least announce it?" Pat whined.

Chet nodded his head, and Pat's face filled with childish excitement.

"CSFBIM drafts running back Priest Holmes first."

Having already agreed on their first and second picks, Gregory & Son wasted no time choosing their players. Gregory the younger, the spitting image of his proud father, weighed in, "We're going with Alexander and Favre."

The two Gregorys, Commish I and Commish II, high-fived each other, all smiles, and the draft continued down the line. Once the Commish laid down his edict mandating fast selections, the draft wrapped up in about an hour.

Junk's selection of Ricky Williams, the AWOL star of the Miami Dolphins who had endorsed the liberal use of marijuana and enthusiastically stated his intention to smoke the "sweet weed" every time he got the chance, headlined as the one of the most bizarre choices of the draft. When CSFBIM pointed out the astronomical odds that Williams would return this year and stated their opinion (in two-part harmony) that Williams was much more likely to spend his fall enriching all the pizza parlors in the greater Miami area than darkening the door of a football stadium, Junk shrugged and stated, "This is the ideal pick under the Chaos Theory™."

Drug offenses aside, the 2004 draft ended in the time-honored striking of side bets, with the usual suspects, Commish, Ladies' Man, Exacta, and Chet Russell, participating. The others usually avoided side bets like the plague. No one seemed to win except Ladies' Man, who had a habit of presenting an invoice for a staggering sum to each of the losers at the annual Super Bowl party.

After the dust settled on the 2004 BIGFFL draft and everyone had struck side bets, it became evident that Buckeye Bob had the most bizarre team ever assembled in the BIGFFL, heavy with long-shot rookies like Roi, last-chance veterans, receiver-eligible tackles, and Browns:

POSITION	PLAYER	TEAM
QB	Attoi Roi	New Orleans
QB	Jeff Garcia	Cleveland
RB	Granite Simms	San Francisco
RB	Lee Suggs	Cleveland
RB	Irving "Pinetop" Nelson	Dallas
RB	Dominic Rhodes	Indianapolis
WR	Kurasawa McGee	Cincinnati
WR	Keenan McCardell	San Diego
WR	Deion Branch	New England
WR	Dennis Northcutt	Cleveland
TE	Jermaine Wiggins	Minnesota
K	Phil Dawson	Cleveland
D	Bears	Chicago
D	Browns	Cleveland
D	49ers	San Francisco
D	Saints	New Orleans
D	Texans	Houston
D	Cardinals	Arizona

As Bob left, he shook the Commish's hand with gusto.

"I tell ya, Bernie, I can't lose this year. I got a great feeling."

"Ya think so, Bob? Well, good luck with that."

After he left, the Commish stared out the window and shook his head, thinking to himself, *Poor Bob. He's really outdone himself this year.*

Little did the Commish suspect that, out of such an unlikely mess of untalented, past-their-prime, has-been players would come a miracle the likes of the 1980 U.S. Hockey Team's Miracle on Ice or Frazier's stunning beating of Ali.

HALFTIME

Week one of the NFL season ... after the Super Bowl, no event matches it for the expectation and excitement it generates in the true NFL junkie. Of course, each fan has a different approach to the Big Day.

The significant others of the BIGFFL owners also had intense reactions to week one. Dread abounded, as they knew their husband or boyfriend would be lost in the football equivalent of the Bermuda Triangle for the duration.

Marty Tanaka, a bachelor, did not have an issue with this. He stocked up on all snack foods known to man, along with plenty of alcohol. He and about a dozen friends would repair to his customized garage-turned-NFL bunker, heavily soundproofed, where Marty had installed four smaller TV sets around a big screen. The smaller sets beamed the lesser games. He had arrayed La-Z-Boy armchairs in rows in the spacious command center, complete with cup holders and TV trays. It was absolute heaven for the NFL enthusiast.

Chet Russell's big day had become problematic. At one time, he would have dropped himself into the couch with a cold one while his wife, Cynthia, left to do some shopping with her girlfriends. However, four children in youth sporting events and various remodeling projects around the house made this direct approach very difficult.

Chet solved this dilemma by buying a house with a large, freestanding RV garage. He maneuvered behind the scenes to make the case that this RV garage should be converted to an entertainment center "for the kids." Toeing this line, while not making the garage available to the kids (at least not at strategic times, like NFL week one), proved a complex and delicate operation.

They purchased the house in April, which Chet thought would give him plenty of time to make the necessary renovations to the RV garage/entertainment center. Unfortunately, the contractors he hired to improve the main house fell behind schedule and couldn't seem to do anything right, at least not to Cynthia's high standards. Chet sweated it down to the last minute, but just hours before NFL Sunday, the contractors put the finishing touches on the entertainment center.

So Chet found himself in a comfortable recliner watching ESPN Sports Center in his very own sanctuary. As Chris Berman began to describe the key matchups for the day, Chet heard a high-pitched scream.

"Daddddddddyyyyyyyyyyy! Mommmmmmmmmmyyyyyyyyyyyyy!"

With a deep sigh, Chet pushed himself out of the luxurious confines of his chair, put on his dad face, and double-timed it back to the house.

It turned out Joanie, one of Chet's twin girls, had skinned her knee, something a little Bactine and a Curad took care of, but it opened the floodgates to a series of events that would succeed in ruining Chet's week one.

The Commish had similar issues at home with children and dogs, but he had adopted a different approach some years ago. Knowing that he wouldn't get in a minute edgewise at the TV set, he gave in and spent the day out and about with the family, doing all of the things they wanted to do. He also used some very valuable features of his digital cable to record the games and sports shows that interested him.

After a long day of activity, the children would be worn out and go to bed early. The Commish would run off to his study, get himself into an 8 AM mindset, and recreate the day. Because he usually stayed up most of the night, he would take Monday off. Mrs. Commish liked this situation because it gave her a night free from snoring and unwanted advances.

Over the years, the Commish, Chet, and other BIGFFL members with family conflicts that could impact football viewing had adopted a number of creative strategies to circumvent these conflicts. A representative list of the most effective strategies included:

1. Telling your wife that you will watch the kids on Sunday so she can indulge herself by going shopping (again) or getting a massage and taking the kids to Peter Piper Pizza (an arcade with TVs) to watch the games, in the process feeding the kids one hundred dollars in tokens to keep them busy while joining the large throng of football fathers gathered around the TV sets.

2. Suggesting that it would be a great day to go to Costco and spending the entire hour there glued to the TVs in the electronics section. Meanwhile, your wife utilizes this valuable time to stock up on various holiday gifts.

3. Barbecuing for three hours straight to watch the key Sunday game on the outdoor TV, cooking enough meat in the process to feed a small army. At the end of the game, it takes a steady assembly line thirty minutes to transport all of the food back into the house for dinner. The family eats barbecue leftovers for weeks during and after the football season.

4. Staying "at work" late four straight Mondays in September, until your wife gets smart, calls the office, blows your cover, and catches you "cheating" at the sports bar.

5. Pushing your daughter on the backyard swing while watching the outside TV mounted at the proper angle for viewing, not realizing she has fallen off until your wife and daughter both start screaming.

6. Checking fantasy stats on the cell phone in church and yelling "Goddamn it!" when you discover your quarterback has thrown three interceptions, much to the dismay of the pastor and parish.

7. Being one of the first on your block to install satellite TV in your SUV to catch all the action on "family trips" from which you just happen to return on Sundays.

8. If completely desperate and out of excuses, offer to do any household chore that keeps you in proximity of a

TV, including folding laundry, vacuuming the family room, cleaning the kitchen, etc.

Of course, the unattached Ladies' Man always played the first week to the hilt. Every year, he jetted to Las Vegas, where he had a deluxe suite at the Bellagio. His elegant approach consisted of watching the games, touring the casino floors, and procuring as much female companionship as possible.

THE THIRD QUARTER

If Bob's preparation for the season appeared somewhat manic, his behavior during week one was downright bizarre.

When Bob came home from the draft, he burst through the door, alarming Rachel, who was sitting at the kitchen table doing bills. Baxter whimpered and left for parts unknown. With his finely honed animal instinct, he knew trouble when he saw it.

"Hi, honey. How was the draft?"

"The draft. It was fabulous. Splendid. I have found the Holy Grail of fantasy football league rosters. The winning combination. The sure thing."

"That's great, honey,"

"That's all you can say? Great? You are about to be the wife of the BIGFFL champion."

"Oh, well in that case, let me go get something nice on for the photographers."

"You're a riot, Alice. Anyway, I'm going upstairs. I have to plot my roster in the computer model and run the first week scenarios. I only have a week to pick a lineup."

On the Saturday night before the games, Bob punched some final permutations into his laptop and hit the print button, thrusting his fist in the air. A piece of paper rolled out of the laser printer, and Bob snapped it up. It contained his final lineup, subject to adjustments once he learned from ESPN Sports Center whether any of his players would be held out because of injury, drug intake, or street violence.

"Yes, this is it," he whispered, his right eye beginning to twitch like a priest in a whorehouse.

Bob's opponent for week one was the Cactus Connection, Marty Tanaka. As Bob typed up his e-mail to submit his lineup, Marty's lineup arrived in Bob's inbox. Marty's lineup consisted of:

POSITION	PLAYER	TEAM
QB	Daunte Culpepper	Minnesota
RB	Edgerrin James	Indianapolis
RB	Corey Dillon	Cincinnati
WR	Randy Moss	Minnesota
WR	Terrell Owens	Philadelphia
TE	Alge Crumpler	Atlanta
K	Mike Vanderjagt	Indianapolis
D	Steelers	Pittsburgh

Bob's lineup was:

POSITION	PLAYER	TEAM
QB	Attoi Roi	New Orleans
RB	Granite Simms	San Francisco
RB	"Pinetop" Nelson	Dallas
WR	Kurasawa McGee	Cincinnati
WR	Keenan McCardell	San Diego
TE	Jermaine Wiggins	Minnesota
K	Phil Dawson	Cleveland
D	Browns	Cleveland

After confirming the lineups, Bob took the stairs two at a time, bounding into the living room. Baxter had taken to giving Bob a wide berth, lying under the kitchen table nestled close to the protection of Rachel's feet, staring out at Bob.

"What are you so happy about?"

"My team."

"Oh, you finally decided who to play."

"Yeah, subject to a few adjustments tomorrow morning, maybe. Say, what are you up to?"

"Just looking at some new recipes in *Cooking Light*."

"Really? How'd you like to go out for a little celebration? Dinner at Pacifica del Mar, a walk on the beach, and who knows what else."

Rachel tried to conceal her surprise. "We haven't done that in a long time. Sounds great."

The next day, Bob won by a wide margin, ninety-eight to sixty-three. Attoi Roi made a spectacular debut, throwing five TD passes and amassing 415 yards. The Browns were classic overachievers, holding their opponents to 146 yards and creating three turnovers, including an interception return for a TD. Things had started off very well for Bob.

Everyone looked forward to the Commish's weekly e-mails following games. The e-mails recapped the results, giving the Commish and the winning teams the opportunity to assert their pimping rights, cramming e-mail boxes full of spam-like material, and proving that most of the owners had very little else to do with their lives.

The Commish exhibited rare form after week one, complimenting Bob's choice of the sleeper Roi and deriding Junk's selection of a lineup that only managed thirty-three points, twenty-two of those from Antonio Gates.

"Worse yet, Junk's other great pick, Ricky Williams, scored three joints, smoked them, and saw God."

Week one gave teams the chance to road test the lineup and get a good idea of the real horses. In week two, they made adjustments to their rosters. For most team owners, this meant diving into the supplemental draft or engineering a trade.

The supplemental draft allowed a team owner to choose any available player or players, as long as his roster did not exceed nineteen after week one and twenty after week two. For a mere five bucks, an owner could add a player to his roster and gather trade bait for down the road.

Trades, on the other hand, often spelled danger in the BIGFFL. Characters like Marty Tanaka and Ladies' Man always tried to take the shirt off your back, while the Commish and CSFBIM prided themselves on being shrewd traders who drove a hard bargain.

Ladies' Man could not be trusted, and for some unknown reason, every year he contacted Slowhand at the beginning of week two to offer his "support" and "assistance" to help "improve" Slowhand's team, usually in the form of a proposed trade.

Like clockwork, Slowhand picked up the phone the Tuesday morning of week two and found Ladies' Man on the other end.

"Yo, Mr. Slowhand. How goes it? I hear you're looking for a trade. I am here to help YOU!"

"Hey, Ladies' Man. Yeah, I'm looking for a quality receiver at this point that I can get points from week in and week out. I would imagine you probably want to hold on to your first-line guys. Thanks for the offer though."

"Tell you what. Since you have Martin and Edge, I'll give you any receiver I have and Fred Taylor for Holmes and one of your WRs. What do you think?"

Silence permeated the line as Slowhand's forehead gathered beads of sweat. Like Charlie Brown trying to kick the football while Lucy held, Slowhand felt himself being lured into the L-Man's web of deceit. In previous years, he would have accepted the trade with only token resistance, but Slowhand had learned his lesson at long last.

"Very tempting, L-Man, but I think I am going to pass this time around. Good luck this week!"

"Let me know if you change your mind."

Not coincidentally, Slowhand and Ladies' Man played each other that very week. It turned out that if Slowhand had accepted the trade, and each team had played the players received through the trade, Ladies' Man would have turned a four-point loss into a two-point victory. The following Tuesday morning, Slowhand received another call from Ladies' Man.

"Yo, Mr. Slowhand. Good thing you didn't trade for my receivers this week. Congrats on your victory this week."

"Thanks, Ladies' Man."

The Commissioner had a challenging job, and it took someone with infinite passion and good humor to get it done. Being the Commish was in Bernie I. Gregory's blood. Under other circumstances, he could have even been a real Commish, perhaps in the NFL or Major League Baseball.

But even someone as good-natured as Bernie could be put to the test. On occasion, two teams could be deadlocked with the same score. In the past, the tie had been broken by pitting the total points of each team's bench against the other. In the current season, the Commish had decided to change the rules to make things a little more interesting. Each team now had to pick a single player to act as his tiebreaker. The Commish had floated the change before the draft and seemed to have achieved consensus, at least Commish-style consensus.

Everyone except Marty Tanaka responded with their opinions. Of course, the new rule came back to sting Marty in week two, and he got on the phone to let the Commish know about it.

"Hey, Bernie. Just wanted to let you know that this new tie-breaking system sucks! We should go with total bench, not one player. I would have won under the reasonable and fair old rule. We should revisit this rule for next year."

"Are you done now, Marty?"

"Yeah, I think so."

"Okay. Point noted!! I would have preferred your criticism during the open exchange of ideas before the draft, when I asked you to weigh in on the new rule, and not after it affects you individually. My other comment is that you might want to rethink your strategy and pick someone other than your second string tight end as your tiebreaker, possibly a quarterback or a running back."

Frustrated and pissed off by petty complaining prompted by the new tie-breaking rule, the Commish spent the rest of the afternoon cranking out and issuing a new edict of Biblical proportions. He called it the "Ten Commandments of the BIGFFL Commissioner."

From: The Commish
To: BIGFFL League Members (Group)
Subject: The Ten Commandments of the BIGFFL Commissioner
Sent: Tue 9/21/2004 6:23 PM

Since you guys have been such whiners, crybabies, and pussies this past week, I have been forced to create and issue the Ten Commandments of the BIGFFL Commissioner. For those of you who are literate (sorry, Marty), please read this carefully. And REMEMBER that this is just a game. In the immortal words of Warren Oates (in his memorable role as Sarge in the Bill Murray comedy *Stripes*), "Lighten up, Francis."

The Ten Commandments of the BIGFFL Commish

1. I shalt throw a mean Perfect Day
2. I shalt oversee a smooth, efficient draft, despite the machinations of Exacta and Junk
3. I shalt fine the crap out of you knuckleheads for various indiscretions
4. I shalt collect cash and be trusted implicitly by my BIGFFL brethren because of my unquestioned honesty and purity of heart (and the fact that I am a CPA)

5. I shalt update the rosters for trades and drafts to the best of my ability, while you pencil dicks remember that I am human

6. I shalt publish and amend the rules of the game at MY discretion, because I know what's best for all of you

7. I shalt make decisions to enable the smooth conduct of league play and resolve any disputes using my compassion and infinite wisdom

8. I shalt not proclaim myself to be a supreme being, although I certainly could qualify as one

9. I shalt not be paid a nickel by you cheap bastards for all the hard work and grief I put up with during the season

10. I (and Mrs. Commish) shalt throw an even meaner Super Bowl party

Okay girls. Time to get back to business and stop worrying so much about the rules.

The Truly Tired of Tending the Nursery Commish

Through all the static and noise, Buckeye Bob began to build himself a season to remember. In week two, he thumped Ladies' Man, scoring seventy-seven points behind another solid week from Attoi Roi, while Ladies' Man had a tough week with only thirty-five points. Bob had never started the season 2-0, and this triggered his superstitious side.

He abandoned science, stowing his computer program and keeping the same lineup in place, afraid to rock the boat.

In week three, he went up against the Commish himself, getting a bad scare in the first quarter when Roi went down. It looked like a bad knee injury, but ended up as only a slight strain. The young phenom came back in the second half to lead Bob's team to a narrow victory 76–72.

Bob crushed the hapless Junkyard Dog in week four, 74–11. Roi had a tough week, as the NFL adjusted to him and his inexperience reading defenses began to show. However, the Browns, playing out of their heads, scored Bob eighteen points, and the unlikely RB combo of Granite Simms and Pinetop Nelson united for forty-three points between them.

And BAM! At the end of week 4, the standings looked like this:

BIGFFL League Standing
Through Week Four

TEAM	Win	Loss	Points For	Points Against	Games Back
Buckeye Bob	4	0	325	181	-
Ladies' Man	3	1	283	275	1
Cactus Connection	3	1	289	281	1
CSFBIM	2	2	268	279	2
Gregory & Son	2	2	262	257	2
Slowhand	1	3	261	302	3
Exacta	1	3	250	288	3
Junkyard Dog	0	4	201	276	4

When Bob came home the Tuesday night after week four, Rachel marveled at the look in his eye and his childlike happiness.

"Guess what, Rach? I am 4–0 and in FIRST PLACE. This calls for a celebration. I've got a cold bottle of Dom in the fridge. I say we open a bottle upstairs in the bedroom and see where it takes us. Baxter, hold down the fort."

Up they went, taking the stairs THREE at a time.

Saturday night, week five. Continuing his superstitious ways, Bob opted to keep his lineup the same. Getting past that major hurdle, Bob and Rachel went to the local Vons to procure game-day supplies.

Bob had a regular routine during the season, especially the food he ate and the beverages he drank. A standard Saturday night shopping list included:

- Original Lays Potato Chips
- Dill dip
- Ranch dip
- One large bag of Tyson Buffalo Strips
- A pint of Haagen Daz Dulce de Leche ice cream
- Rib eye steaks (2) for the barbecue
- Bush's barbecue baked beans
- Bag of red potatoes and ingredients for Bob's specialty potato salad
- A case of Diet Coke
- A six-pack of Miller Lite (NOT Bud!)

After bringing home the supplies, Bob prepared the potato salad and cleaned the barbecue grill for the steaks. They finished the evening on the couch, watching *Saturday Night Live* and falling asleep before it ended.

Early Sunday morning, Bob arose from a restless night's sleep, leaving Rachel to doze a little longer. The night before, he dreamed that he coached a real NFL team, but all of his players stood less than three feet tall and a talking opossum quarterbacked the team. Because of their size, they couldn't stop the other team from scoring, so they had to keep pace with the other team and hope they got the ball first. It was their good fortune to win the coin toss eight times out of ten, defying the odds. On top of that, tackling them was almost impossible, the opossum had a fantastic arm and he could read defenses like a champ, so they usually won. Bob had no idea what the dream meant, but he took it as a good omen.

He powered on the computer, looking for an e-mail from Chet and Pat of CSFBIM, his opponent for the week. Sure enough, it sat in his inbox, detailing their lineup for the week and containing the obligatory trash talk. He responded with his lineup.

To complete his Sunday ritual, Bob logged on to ESPN.com to check the injury situation. With his lineup confirmed, Bob went downstairs and found Rachel making scrambled eggs and toast. Happy with Bob's mood of late, Baxter bounded up to him, accepted some ear scratching and vigorous petting, and trotted off to his food bowl.

Bob grabbed the remote and switched on the two TVs. He had installed the second before the season so he could watch multiple games at the same time. FOX had the first game of the day, the New Orleans Saints against the Buffalo Bills. He liked that, because it would give him a good indication of how he would do right away. He arrived just in time to catch a brief interview with his QB, Attoi Roi.

"To what do you attribute your tremendous success in your first year as an NFL quarterback?"

"Hair spray. If my hair stays in place, I can't lose. It keeps my head and my brain clear."

Bob and Rachel, who sometimes watched the games with Bob, laughed.

"Who is this clown?"

"Hey, hey, hey. That guy's no clown. He's my quarterback."

"Oh."

Roi now explained the origin of his hair spray. "It's my own mixture. I make it and can it myself. I call it Essence of Attoi. My agent, Max Brenneman, is working on a contract to mass produce it."

"On a more serious note, what do you expect from the tough Buffalo defense today, and how do you plan to counter it?"

"I'm just going to play my game. Everything else will take care of itself."

"What about the blitz? They blitz on almost every down and their head coach has stated he is going to try to capitalize on your inexperience."

"I throw too fast to worry about the blitz. They can't get to me fast enough. Hey, can we take a minute. I want to say hi to my mom. Hi, Mom! I also want to mention that I am wearing Nike shoes, the official sponsor of Attoi Roi."

"Anything else you'd like to mention?"

"Nah. That should do it for now."

"One final question, Attoi. You seem to be known around the clubhouse as a funny guy and a practical joker of sorts. Is that true?"

"Oh, yeah. I love to have a good time. Someday, after my career is over, I think I'll be a standup comedian or a movie star. I got the gift, baby."

"Thank you Attoi, and good luck today."

"Thanks."

The camera caught Roi going into a funky dance, a cross between the Ickey Shuffle and John Travolta's disco moves from *Saturday Night Fever*, just as the network cut to a commercial.

Just then, the phone rang.

"Honey, it's Bernie."

"Thanks, Rach. Hey, Bernie. What's up?"

"I just wanted to let you know that I'm levying a fine on you for that interview your QB just gave. And another fine for that weird dance at the end. What was that all about?"

"Don't know, Commish. Don't care as long as he keeps performing well."

"Well, fifteen bucks is coming out of your account. Five dollars for the interview and ten dollars for that god-awful dance."

"Fine with me. There'll be plenty of cash in there at the end of the year to absorb it. Good luck in your game. Who're you playing again?"

"Junk. Should be a piece of cake."

"Oh yeah. Take it easy, Bernie."

"You too, Bob."

The game plodded along, uneventful through the first quarter and ending in a scoreless deadlock. Early in the second quarter, the Saints, starting on their own fifteen yard line, got something going. Roi ran a QB draw, going right up behind the center and finding a seam that carried him to the twenty-eight. On the next play, he rolled out right, drilling a fourteen-yard strike to his tight end, Ernie Conwell. After a couple of five yard spurts by Deuce McAllister, Roi settled into a five-step drop, got perfect protection from his line, and launched a forty-eight-yard missile on a rope to Donte' Stallworth, who, with the ball pulled in for a score, trotted over to the crowd, took a Sharpie from his agent, signed the ball, and handed it over for a quick sale on eBay using the agent's laptop.

"Oooooo, yeah! What a pass!!!"

Bob executed a happy dance, twirling around and pumping his fist. Baxter didn't like this at all and stood by the door, begging to be let out to the backyard.

"Did you see that, Rach? And he threw it to Stallworth, not Horn. No points for CSFBIM!!!"

In the third quarter, with the Saints up seventeen to fourteen on another Roi TD toss and a field goal, the Saints intercepted a Drew Bledsoe duck and returned the ball to the Bills' thirty-four yard line. The Saints trotted onto the field, two wide receivers on either side of the formation, and sent them long. Roi rolled left, planted himself to throw, and airmailed a beauty in the direction of Donte' Stallworth. The ball floated down, touched Stallworth's fingertips, and slid right through, dropping to the ground. The Bills took a time-out.

"Damn! That son of a bitch Stallworth is worthless. He just cost me nine points."

"But you loved him earlier in the game."

"I know, but, you see, well, it's complicated, that's all."

"Yes, I see that. Well, I'm going shopping. Enjoy the rest of the game."

"What? Oh yeah. I'll see you later. We'll get the steaks on about four thirty, after the afternoon game."

After the time-out, the Saints came out in a two-back formation, with the Deuce in the tailback position. Roi faked a handoff to the Deuce, took a deep drop, and threw a well-executed screen pass to where the Deuce had settled in. The play took the Bills by surprise. The Deuce sprinted into open field, cut back right, and made it to the one yard line before being pushed out of bounds by the free safety.

"Yes!! Now, time for a QB sneak or a short pass!"

Bob jumped to his feet and began pacing back and forth. As he watched, Roi handed off to the Deuce, who went over the center-right guard hole, got airborne, and scored the touchdown.

"Shit, shit, shit! That should have been mine. Son of a bitch Stallworth!"

The Bills kicked another field goal in the fourth quarter, but the Saints managed the clock well with an effective running game, taking most of the time off before the Bills could get the ball again. A last minute drive ended without a score. Final score: Saints, twenty-four; Bills, seventeen.

Although Roi had not scored as much as usual, he still managed to get twenty-four points. By his count, Bob looked pretty good against the meager points CSFBIM had managed so far.

In the afternoon matchups, Bob had Irving "Pinetop" Nelson going. Pinetop led his Dallas Cowboys to 45–7 victory over the hapless Arizona Cardinals. Along the way, he scored four TDs, threw for another, and racked up 210 total yards for a total of forty-four points for Bob. Rachel came through the door just as the final gun sounded on the game, arms full of bags filled with shoes and clothes.

"Maybe I shouldn't let you go out shopping by yourself. You're going to spend all of my winnings."

"That's the idea. Besides, I needed shoes."

"Yeah, right. Don't you already have forty-three pair of black shoes and forty-one pair of brown?"

"Fifty-one pair and forty-nine pair, respectively, which is not nearly enough. So, how'd it go?"

"Couldn't have gone better. I'm up on CSFBIM by thirty-nine points, and he's only got his kicker left to play tonight. Looks like another win. I'm five and oh."

"Congratulations. Now, how about those steaks? All that hard work shopping made me very hungry."

"Chow down on some buffalo strips. I'll get the coals started."

The incredible juggernaut continued. Week six, facing Slowhand, Roi and company rolled to a BIGFFL record 148 points, while Slowhand managed an embarrassing thirteen points. In week seven, completing the first tour through the league, Bob survived a close call from Exacta, who had been struggling but rode a rejuvenated Marshall Faulk to a season-high seventy-eight points. Bob needed a last-second field goal by his kicker Brown to eke out a 79–78 victory.

Week eight brought a marquee match up between Bob and Marty Tanaka, his closest competition. Going into the week, the standings were:

BIGFFL League Standing
Through Week Seven

TEAM	Win	Loss	Points For	Points Against	Games Back
Buckeye Bob	7	0	590	460	-
Cactus Connection	5	2	485	466	2
Ladies' Man	4	3	544	412	3
CSFBIM	3	4	512	477	4
Gregory & Son	3	4	498	510	4
Slowhand	3	4	449	499	4
Exacta	3	4	398	486	5
Junkyard Dog	0	7	346	512	7

In a low-scoring game, Marty's QB Culpepper and Bob's QB Roi matched interceptions and both defenses collapsed, scoring negative numbers. When the dust settled on Monday night, Bob and Marty remained in a dead heat, 38–38, coming down to the tiebreaker. Bob had selected Drew Brees as his tiebreaker, the Charger QB who had been an extreme long shot at the beginning of the year but had come into his own. He had a great week, scoring twenty-seven points. Marty forgot to pick a tiebreaker, so it would not have mattered unless Brees had not played or had scored zero or less points.

Of course, Marty called the Commish, at home this time, to rant about the tiebreaker.

"Hey, Commish-in-Error. I renew my objection to the current system of breaking ties. It's fucked up, and I think we should go back to the old system next year.

"Listen, Cactus Head, you're the asshole who forgot to pick his tiebreaker. If you had won this week, you would have been squarely behind the new rule. Request denied. We're staying with the new system. And stop calling me at home."

Motivated by Marty's irate comments, the Commish sent out a scathing midseason report card, giving Cactus Connection a D+, praising Buckeye Bob for his great start, and warning that if he heard another word about tiebreakers, he would hunt down and kill the source with extreme prejudice.

Weeks nine and ten constituted more of the same for Bob, and he coasted into week eleven with a commanding lead:

BIGFFL League Standing
Through Week Ten

TEAM	Win	Loss	Points For	Points Against	Games Back
Buckeye Bob	10	0	803	615	-
Ladies' Man	7	3	688	637	3
CSFBIM	5	5	703	698	5
Gregory & Son	5	5	692	714	5
Cactus Connection	5	5	657	622	5
Slowhand	4	6	584	625	6
Exacta	4	6	502	512	6
Junkyard Dog	0	10	451	657	10

COMMERCIAL BREAK

On week eleven, Bob got home around 6 PM on Wednesday evening, and he and Rachel took their customary walk with Baxter. Bob loved fall, his favorite time of year, and he especially loved these walks. The air felt crisp and cool. The trees shed leaves of orange, yellow, and brown. He had a 10–0 record in the BIGFFL. Life was good. No, life was great.

When they got home from their walk, Bob took a quick shower and logged onto the computer to check ESPN news. Right away, he saw the headline "ROI AWOL." In a panic, he clicked on the link and read the article.

ROI AWOL
By Nipper Collins
STAFF WRITER

The Saints reported today that their outstanding young rookie quarterback Attoi Roi is AWOL and they have no

idea of his whereabouts. He was last seen leaving the Saints'
practice complex in his new Lincoln Navigator Tuesday
night. In a prepared statement, TR Nusbaum, a spokes-
person for the Saints' executive management, reported:

"We are currently trying to establish the location of Attoi
Roi, who has not requested a leave and has not been
seen since Tuesday night. We are confident we will deter-
mine his whereabouts in time for this week's game and
will report further details as they become available."

Rumors have Roi sighted at the New Orleans
International Airport on his way to parts unknown.
However, these rumors are unsubstantiated.

There was a follow up article that sounded even worse.

SAINTS MAKE CONTACT WITH ROI
By Nipper Collins
STAFF WRITER

In a bizarre twist on the Attoi Roi story, the Saints have
published a second press release stating that they have made
positive contact with Attoi Roi, their prize rookie quarter-
back, who leads the NFL in quarterback ratings with 132.

"Mr. Roi contacted us at 10:56 PM eastern standard time. It
was a short phone call, during which Mr. Roi indicated that,
on his agent's advice, he has retired from football to pursue
a career in baseball. He is currently in Louisville, Kentucky,

where he plans to work out with the Louisville Sporting Woods, a semipro team sponsored by Hillerich and Bradsby, while he prepares for spring training with the Los Angeles Dodgers, the team that Roi previously turned down when they made him their number one draft pick out of college."

When the Saints representative reminded Roi that he had a contract to finish the season with the Saints and may face legal repercussions if he fails to do so, Roi stated:

"Who gives a f**k about that? That's chump change. I'll pay them back out of the interest on my $10 million signing bonus with the Dodgers. Anyway, my agent, Tyrone Rico, has never steered me wrong before. He convinced me that base-ball is much better for me in the long run because I can make much more money, and my risk of injury is much lower."

When asked about next steps, the Saints' representative did not comment. He did, however, confirm that they had sus-pended Roi until further notice and would be starting Slappy Kendall, Roi's backup and the Saints' fifth round pick in the 2003 draft, against the first place Baltimore Ravens.

"Well, this is certainly fucked. The only QB that I can pick up now is Testaverde, and he's a steaming pile."

After thinking about his other options, trades, or supplemental picks, Bob decided it was a lost cause and just stared at the screen in shock. After about a minute, he reached down, opened the bottom right drawer of his desk and pulled out a dusty half-full bottle of Jack

Daniels and a shot glass. He set the shot glass in front of him, poured three fingers, and downed it in a gulp. After he let the whisky settle, he got up, grabbed his car keys, and walked down the stairs and out the door, passing Rachel and Baxter without a word or a glance. Rachel stared at the door as it closed.

By the time she decided to go after him to find out what was going on, he was already pulling out of the driveway, leaving a trail of burned rubber in his wake.

She ran up to the office, saw the empty shot glass and the bottle of Jack and noticed the ESPN article. The next thing she did was to pick up the phone.

"This is Robert."

"Hi, Robert. This is Rachel."

"Hey, Rachel. What's up?"

"Bob just left the house without a word. When I went up to his office, I saw a bottle of Jack Daniels on the desk and an article about his quarterback, Attoi Roy. I think he went down to his old hangout, O'Bryan's Pub. I'm worried about him, and I thought you might be able to talk some sense into him. I never could when he gets like this."

"I don't know if I can do any better than you can, Rachel, but I can give it a try. Is it that place over by the 7-11 and the Carl's Jr.?"

"Yeah."

"I can get over there in about thirty minutes."

"Thank you so much, Robert."

When Ladies' Man got to O'Bryan's, he found Bob at the back of the bar on a stool drinking shots of Bushmills, staring straight ahead, and mumbling. When he sat down, Bob didn't notice him.

After about a minute, Ladies' Man tried to rouse Bob from his trance. "Hey there, Bob. How's it going?"

Bob didn't say anything at first. After he finished his latest shot, he banged it down on the table, turned to Bernie, and slurred, "How's it going? How's it going. I'll tell you how it's going. That goddamn fuckin' Roi is going to ruin my season. That's how it's going. Bartender, another Bushmills. You want anything, Ladies' Man?"

"No thanks, Bob. I haven't heard the news. What happened?"

"Bottom line, Roi fucked me royal. He's run off to be a baseball player. A fucking baseball player! There goes my chance at the trophy. And it was going so well."

Ladies' Man raised an eyebrow and scratched his head.

"Wow. Tough luck, Bob. But hey, it's just a game. Try not to take it so hard."

"Yeah, that's easy for you to say Ladies' Man. You've won the BIGFFL a few times. I never have. I want to win, just once, so I can prove to everyone that I understand this game and I know how to put together a good team."

"Bob, no one understands this game. Sure, I've won, but it's just blind luck. Just think about what we do. We draft twenty players each year, and who knows if any of them will do well. Shit, you've seen how many guys go down to injury in week one. And face it, if it's your marquee player, you're screwed. Or someone goes off and smokes dope and gets suspended. Or there's a car crash or an assault. It's all luck, and just because I've won it a few times doesn't mean anything. Everyone has a lot of respect for you in this league, whether you win or not. Sure, you get ribbed, but that happens to everyone. It's all part of the fun. If no one trash talked you, that's when you should start worrying. And besides, drinking all the whisky in the world isn't going to help the situation."

Bob had picked up his shot and was about to drain it. Instead, he put it back down. After a moment, he looked at Ladies' Man.

"You know, you're right. What the hell am I doing? I have a great life, Rachel, Baxter. And I have all you guys. And just think. We can do this bullshit the rest of our lives."

"Damn right, Bob. Now, are you gonna be okay, or do I need to get you a suite at the Betty Ford Clinic?"

"Nah. I think I'm gonna be okay. Hell, I don't need Roi. I've got a three game lead with six to go. In fact, while I've been sitting here getting wasted, I came up with a new strategy. I'm tired of playing the same guys. It's time to crank up the computer program again and come up with some *new choices*. I think I'll heat up the waiver wire and make some *moves*."

"That's great. Good to see you back in the game. Well, why don't I drive you home? You can pick up your car tomorrow morning."

Bob got up and shook Ladies' Man's hand.

"Yeah, thanks L-Man. You're the best."

THE FOURTH QUARTER

With his resurrected computer program, Bob made some adjustments to the assumptions, input the season-to-date stats, and ran some different scenarios. Deciding not to discard the lineup that had taken him to first place, he instead traded his bench players or dropped them and drafted new players in their place, with the guiding principle that they must be current or former Cleveland Browns.

For a sanity check, Bob called Ladies' Man to explain his strategy and get his input.

"Hey, Ladies' Man, you got a minute? I want to run my new lineup by you and see what you think."

"Sure, Bob. Hit me."

Thirty minutes later, Bob concluded, "I'm from Cleveland. They're my team, and they've never let me down before. How can I lose?"

To which Ladies' Man simply replied, "If you were from Berlin, would you start the Gestapo at all your positions?"

Bob ignored that comment, as well as the unfortunate fact that the Browns HAD let him down before without fail. When the dust settled, his lineup consisted of:

POSITION	PLAYER	TEAM
QB	Jeff Garcia	Cleveland
RB	Lee Suggs	Cleveland
RB	William Green	Cleveland
WR	Dennis Northcutt	Cleveland
WR	Antonio Bryant	Cleveland
TE	Steve Heiden	Cleveland
K	Phil Dawson	Cleveland
D	Browns	Cleveland

When Junkyard Dog, Bob's week eleven opponent, received Bob's lineup, he read it with admiration.

"This is the most pure use of the Chaos Theory™ I've ever seen. Why didn't I think of that?"

The retooled Buckeye Bobs took the field against the 0–10 Junkyard Dogs. Everyone watched to see if Bob would go 11–0 or Junk would crack the win column and become 1–10.

Bob's team played well and put up respectable numbers, sixty-one points in all. However, Junk's team played out of its head, putting up ninety-five points with his star tight end Antonio Gates contributing twenty-six points alone. At the end of the day, both teams had ended their streaks. Still, Bob felt optimistic.

"You know, Rach, I feel good about this new lineup. Sixty-one points is pretty decent. Hell, it's better than most of the lineups I've had in past years. And I finally get a chance to indulge my fantasy to play all Brownies. You watch. They'll take care of me."

"Whatever you say, Bob. I'm just happy to see you smiling again."

Bob continued to lose and the lead slipped away, but he no longer cared. In fact, the smile on his face got bigger and bigger. He had the all-Brownie team he had always wanted, but they just didn't have the firepower to average more than about fifty to fifty-five points a week, and with some of the other teams in the league scoring seventy-five to one hundred, that just didn't cut it. After the Monday night game ended on week fifteen, Bob found he had lost to Exacta fifty-two to forty-nine and had fallen to 10–5.

During Bob's losing streak, Marty Tanaka's Cactus Connection heated up, stringing together convincing victories with impressive scores like 125 and 133 points, and he had done the opposite of Bob, winning five in a row. When Bob accessed the BIGFFL Web site on Tuesday morning, he saw these standings:

BIGFFL League Standing
Through Week Fifteen

TEAM	Win	Loss	Points For	Points Against	Games Back
Buckeye Bob	10	5	1056	1003	-
Cactus Connection	10	5	1049	957	-
CSFBIM	9	6	1055	1025	1
Ladies' Man	9	6	1017	1008	1
Gregory & Son	8	7	981	1001	2
Exacta	6	9	912	888	4
Slowhand	5	10	933	973	5
Junkyard Dog	3	12	849	997	7

As he pored over the situation, Bob realized that the Great Brownie Experiment had been fun, but it had also been an absolute failure. He decided to reinstate his old lineup, but in a final nod to the Browns, he considered drafting forty-one-year old Vinny Testaverde to shore up the QB spot in week sixteen. Testaverde was a one-time Brown currently playing decent ball for the Dallas Cowboys and the only viable starter available on the free agent list. The recent deterioration of Garcia's game had left him little alternative. When he clicked the BIGFFL Web site analysis of the week's games, it surprised him to see Roi's name in the headlines again.

Roi to Return QB Controversy Looms
By Nipper Collins
STAFF WRITER

In another stunning twist in the Attoi Roi saga, Roi has realized that football is the game for him and has indicated his desire to return to the Saints, effective immediately. The Saints could not be reached for comment and have only issued a terse statement confirming this announcement.

Asked about his abrupt change of heart, Roi stated "My f**kin' agent steered me wrong, the dishonest f**k. I fired his ass. Beyond that, I miss football and I think the Saints can use me. They have played very well this season and they have an excellent chance to win the division. With me, they have a better chance to realize that goal."

Detractors of Roi have speculated that Roi's money has run out. Regardless, the football world will now wait

> *to learn how the Saints organization will resolve this*
> *quarterback controversy, made more difficult because of*
> *the excellent play of Slappy Kendall in Roi's absence.*

Bob ran this new development through his brain. His heart told him to go with Roi, though he did not know whether the Saints would put Roi back in or continue to go with the unlikely hero Slappy Kendall. His head told him to draft and play Testaverde, who would start and put up respectable numbers. Bob split the difference, drafting Testaverde, dropping Garcia, and opting to gather some additional intelligence. He would make a final decision just before game time.

NFL Sunday, week sixteen, the final week of the BIGFFL season, dawned as another gorgeous fall morning in San Diego. Bob made himself a cup of coffee and booted up the computer.

The Saints had not made his quarterback decision any easier, refusing to comment all week and leaving it open to speculation as to who the starting quarterback would be. The Saints told the press they would make a game-time decision on who would start. They did not rule out playing both quarterbacks during the game.

Bob went down to turn on the TV. He thought if he could watch the pregame warm-ups, he might get an indication of who would start, but both Kendall and Roi took an equal amount of snaps and he had no better idea of who would start as kickoff time approached.

At 9:55 AM, Bob went up and completed his lineup selection. In the meantime, he had received an e-mail from Marty Tanaka, his opponent in this critical final week game, with the lineup of:

POSITION	PLAYER	TEAM
QB	Daunte Culpepper	Minnesota
RB	Edgerrin James	Indianapolis
RB	Corey Dillon	Cincinnati
WR	Randy Moss	Minnesota
WR	Terrell Owens	Philadelphia
TE	Alge Crumpler	Atlanta
K	Mike Vanderjagt	Indianapolis
D	Steelers	Pittsburgh

Bob's lineup was:

POSITION	PLAYER	TEAM
QB	Attoi Roi	New Orleans
RB	Granite Simms	San Francisco
RB	"Pinetop" Nelson	Dallas
WR	Kurasawa McGee	Cincinnati
WR	Keenan McCardell	San Diego
TE	Jermaine Wiggins	Minnesota
K	Kris Brown	Houston
D	Browns	Cleveland

Bob walked back downstairs to watch the Saints-49ers game. The Saints won the coin toss and elected to receive. The 49ers kicker booted the ball deep to the Saints three yard line. The Saints kick returner, Michael Lewis, fielded the ball and took off toward the wall forming on his right. He peeled up behind his blockers, completing a respectable return to the thirty-eight yard line. Bob held his breath, hoping his intuition would prove accurate and waiting to see who would come onto the field—Kendall or Roi.

"Damn!"

Bob smacked his fist into the palm of his hand as he saw Kendall trot out and huddle up the team. The camera panned to Roi, who sat on the bench near the Gatorade cooler, all alone.

Rachel, drying dishes in the kitchen, dropped her towel and came into the living room, sitting on the arm of Bob's chair and touching his hair.

"What's wrong, Bob? Are you okay?"

"I'm fine. It's just that it doesn't look like Roi is going to play, and I started him instead of Testaverde. I just gotta remember it's a game. It could all work out yet."

With no other players going in the Saint game, Bob decided to switch to the Vikings-Steelers game to check on the progress of Marty's quarterback. If Culpepper had one of his big days, Bob couldn't match up. Not having a quarterback gave away thirty or more points, which would be almost insurmountable. If Culpepper had a tough day or at least threw a few interceptions to offset the touchdowns and yardage, he might still have a chance.

As Bob watched Culpepper, he noticed that the Steelers seemed to have his run and scramble contained and they had Randy Moss's number. As the first half ended, Culpepper only had one TD, an interception, and seventy-six total yards, translating to only three fantasy points. If Culpepper had a similar second half, Bob could still contend.

At halftime, Bob switched back to the Saints game. Kendall remained at the helm and he continued to have an excellent game. He had two TDs and 189 yards for fifteen points. Roi's chances of entering the game started to look pretty slim.

The Steelers defense treated Culpepper to more of the same in the second half. At the end of the third quarter, Culpepper had remained ineffective, throwing for only forty-two more yards and another interception. His point total had been reduced to zero, and he showed no signs of figuring out the tough Steeler defense.

Bob surfed his way back to the Saints game. Onscreen, he saw a group of Saints huddled around a player. The game had been stopped. The FOX cameras cut to another angle, and Bob saw Kendall's name on the back of the injured player's jersey. As they waited for further information, the FOX announcers speculated on the injury.

"Well, Dick, it could be a couple of different things. It looked like his knee took a pretty wicked bend when he got hit, but the other guy clocked him pretty good to the head."

"Yes, Ron. I think he might have actually been knocked out cold for a moment."

"Well, he's awake now and seems to be talking to the trainer. It looks like they are going to hoist him up. His eyes look blank. Might be a concussion."

"Whatever it is, I don't think he's in any shape to return. Looks like they are going to have to go to the prodigal son, Attoi Roi. I don't think Roi would have wanted to get his opportunity to get back in the lineup this way, but here he comes."

Bob sat stunned as Roi strapped on his helmet and gathered the team. One minute, fifty-nine seconds to go in the third quarter. Saints down 34–24. Roi would have an entire quarter to put some points on the board for Bob.

The first play out of the gate, Roi faked a handoff to Aaron Stecker, looked like he would go out to the flat for a short pass, and turned to his right, drilling a low line-drive to Joe Horn, who streaked down the right sideline. Horn caught the ball in stride and streaked into the end zone. With the extra point, the score stood at 34–31.

When they got the ball back, the 49ers kept the ball on the ground and began to eat up the clock. After over seven minutes of possession, they had reached the Saints' fourteen yard line. They ran three more plays, keeping the ball out of the air, and settled for a field goal. It was 37–31. Seven minutes, forty-five seconds to go. The Saints needed a touchdown to win.

Confident that they could drive against the marginal 49ers defense, Roi and the Saints coaching staff decided to play high percentage football and give the ball to the Deuce and Aaron Stecker. The two backs ate up yardage, going from their own eighteen to the 49ers' nine in 6:55. With fifty seconds on the clock, they needed a touchdown to tie and an extra point to win. They could not get a first down, so they had four downs to score, with two timeouts left. Running the ball would be risky at this point, so they needed to pass the ball into the end zone.

First down. Roi took a quick drop and tried to hit Ernie Conwell on a crossing pattern. The 49ers middle linebacker reacted and batted it down. Second down. Roi took another quick drop, saw Donte' Stallworth and lofted the ball to the corner of the end zone. Stallworth caught it, but his left foot landed out of bounds. Third down. Roi handed the ball to the Deuce, who fought hard and willed the ball down to the four. Fourth down. Roi let the clock run down to twenty-five seconds before calling timeout. That left them one just in case they scored the TD and had any problems during the extra point.

On the sidelines, Roi and Coach Donovan Gage conferred, trying to determine the right play to get past the suddenly tough 49ers defense. Slappy Kendall joined the conversation, slapping at bugs on his uniform that only he could see. Deciding on a play, Donovan Gage sent his rookie QB back into the game.

"Just use your instincts. You'll be fine."

Roi called the play and stepped up to center.

"Red twenty-three. Red twenty-three. Hut. Hut hut. Hut."

The ball nestled in his hands as he stepped right, rolling out toward the sideline. He first looked to Joe Horn, but the 49er free safety had Horn blanketed. Because of the short field, Roi did not have time for a second look. Instead, he tucked the ball up under his right arm and took off running, his long legs striding toward the end zone. He juked one 49er defender, who missed him completely, glanced off a second, and pushed off hard at about the two yard line, launching himself into the air and clearing the last 49er between him and the goal line. As he came back down to earth, he fell, rolled, and came up in the end zone, ball raised in the air.

The crowd celebrated with a deafening roar, but the officials had not yet signaled touchdown. Instead, they had gathered in the right corner of the end zone, conferring among themselves. After about a minute, the referee emerged from the huddle and addressed the restless crowd.

"The ruling on the field is that the player's knee touched the ground before the ball broke the plane of the goal line. The play is under review by officials in the booth."

The crowd booed and threw all sorts of debris onto the field. Roi, who had been hovering around the officials during their conference, ran over to the referee to plead his case. Bob stood in front of the TV set, arguing with Baxter.

"Did you see that play, boy? That was a no-brainer. He was over the line easy. I'm sure they'll overturn it. Oh, man."

For his part, Baxter maintained a healthy distance between himself and his owner.

After the two minutes allotted for the review, the officials in the booth called down their final ruling to the referee. A hush came over the stadium as the referee stepped onto the field.

At this point, his microphone went dead. One of the Saints' assistants ran onto the field and inserted some new batteries into the power pack. Giving the referee the thumbs up, he ran back off the field.

"After further review, it has been determined conclusively that the player's knee did *not* touch the ground before the ball crossed the plane of the goal line. Touchdown, New Orleans."

The place exploded. After the grounds crew cleaned up the piles of trash accumulated on the field, the Saints returned to the field to settle the not-so-small matter of the extra point. The kick split the uprights and the Saints won thirty-eight to thirty-seven.

Bob bounded up the stairs and logged onto the BIGFFL Web site. He and Marty were tied 87–87. It would come down to Marty's tiebreaker, Bulger, the St. Louis Rams' QB playing Monday night against the Tampa Bay Buccaneers, against Bob's tiebreaker, Vinny Testaverde, who had an excellent game on Sunday night, scoring a season-high twenty-eight points. Ironically, if they had played under the old tiebreaker rule, Marty would have already won because his bench would have easily beaten the mostly Browns bench Bob now had on his roster. As it stood, Marty needed a formidable twenty-eight points from Bulger, who had been averaging closer to fourteen, to win.

The following evening, Marty tuned in to the Monday night game with little, if any, hope that Bulger would come through. Bob opted to go out to dinner with Rachel and see what happened when he came home.

As the pregame commentary ended and the kicker teed up the football for the opening kickoff, Marty paced back and forth, a basket case. Luckily for Marty, Bulger started out well and already had eighteen fantasy league points at halftime. In the second half, the Bucs defense adjusted and held Bulger to forty-five yards, enough to net Marty three more points, up to twenty-one. Midway through the fourth quarter, Bulger threw another TD. With the additional yardage, he now had thirty points, and the Rams led 28–21. Marty just about had it nailed!

The Bucs took possession of the ball at their own twenty-three. With three timeouts, they still had plenty of time to score and they proceeded to do so, knotting it up at 28–28 with thirty-five seconds left. As this last score developed, Marty began to address the TV like an old friend. When the Bucs scored, he resumed his pacing.

"Steady now. Steady. Let's sit on the ball and take it into OT. No need to take any unnecessary risks."

He still had the victory as long as the Rams didn't do anything stupid. The Bucs kicker kept the ball low on the kickoff, a line drive that was caught by the up back, who caught a seam and spurted all the way to the Bucs forty-three.

"Ah, shit. Those assholes are going to think they can get in field goal range, but they don't have enough time to run it there. They'll have to throw."

The Rams clapped out of the huddle and set up in a pass formation. Bulger took a five step drop, faked left, and looked right, tossing the ball with pinpoint precision to his receiver, Isaac Bruce, who ran a slant pattern. The ball squeaked through the paper thin opening between the Bucs' linebacker and Bruce. Just as Bruce wrapped his hands around the ball, he took a ferocious hit from two separate Bucs arriving at the same time. The ball popped lose, orbiting above the playing field and then settling into the hands of the Bucs' linebacker, who tucked it away for the interception and took advantage of a seam to run the ball back for a touchdown.

Just like that, the Bucs had averted overtime and won the game. In the process, Bulger's interception had cost Marty three points, just enough to push him back to twenty-seven points, one point shy of Buckeye Bob.

"Ahhhhhhh."

An animal scream pierced the night, as Marty took his remote and launched it, scoring a direct hit on the far wall and leaving a big black gash.

Bob and Rachel came back around 10 P.M., oblivious to the outcome of the game. In the darkness of the kitchen, Bob saw the message light on the answering machine blinking and the number 4, signifying four new messages.

"How the hell did we get four messages? We were only gone for a little while."

Rachel just shrugged her shoulders, as did Baxter.

Bob tapped the message button.

From Bernie: "Congratulations BIGFFL Champion. What a way to win!"

From Ladies' Man: "Yo, Buckeye Bob. Nice comeback. Sweet victory."

From CSFBIM: "Way to go, Bob! You kicked ol' Cactus up one side and down the other. You've got pimping rights now for a whole season. Use 'em well!"

From Mom: "Hi, honey. I just called to
say hello. Everything's fine here. Say hi
to Rachel for me. Love you, bye."

Bob couldn't believe it. He ran up to his office so he could see the final score with his own eyes. Sure enough, he had won the game! He ran back down the stairs, making an unearthly racket.

"Yeeeeeeheeeeeeeeee. Yeah baby!"

Baxter let out a yowl and hightailed it up the stairs as Bob bearhugged Rachel and kissed her. As they embraced each other, they jumped up and down.

"I did it, Rach! I finally did it!"

Tears of joy fell from Bob's eyes as he pulled Rachel to him again and held her close. Bob had won the BIGFFL championship!

The next evening, Bob sat in his office checking out the e-mail from the Commish announcing his victory. He awakened from his reverie when he heard Rachel's voice from down the hall.

"Hey, Bob? Dinner's ready. Baxter and I are waiting."

At the same time she walked through the doorway, Baxter bounded past her, leapt onto Bob's lap, and licked his face, depositing dog slobber on Bob's cheek.

"Down, Baxter. Hey, Rach, check out this e-mail. I've finally arrived."

Rachel leaned over and read the e-mail as Bob scrolled down. When she finished, she put her arms around Bob's neck and kissed him. In the process, Bob pulled her onto his lap.

"Hey, champ, what about dinner?"

"It'll keep. Time to claim my prize for winning the championship. Why don't we adjourn to the bedroom for the award ceremony?"

"Okay!"

For the next half hour, Baxter sat at the closed bedroom door, knowing they would eventually emerge, as they always did, to feed him.

In the weeks leading up to Super Bowl Sunday, Bob acted like a little kid on Christmas Eve, his excitement and impatience building every day. When the big day arrived, he couldn't sleep and got up early, careful not to wake Rachel.

He booted up the computer to check his e-mail and peruse ESPN. After reading through the latest Super Bowl developments, Bob fed Baxter, showered, and got dressed. He and his friend Chuck were observing their annual ritual of breakfast at Perry's Diner. Bob only went to Perry's twice a year, before the Perfect Day and before the Super Bowl, counting it as one of the culinary highlights of the year.

Rachel tended the garden in the backyard. She wore her cutoff jean shorts, Bob's old red polo shirt, and sun hat. She had dirt smeared across her forearms and cheek.

"The lavender looks great. I'm leaving to pick up Chuck and head down to Perry's. What are you and Lori up to?"

"We're going to see a movie, have lunch, and do some shopping."

"You should pick up some more shoes. I don't think you have enough."

"Good idea. I think I will."

Bob leaned over and kissed Rachel good-bye, lingering for a moment and stroking her cheek.

"See you later. Around eight or so."

"Have fun with your bragging rights."

"Pimping rights."

"Right, pimping rights."

"Bye."

After Bob and Chuck gorged themselves at Perry's and visited Polar Golf to check out the newest clubs and other golf equipment on the market, Bob dropped Chuck off at his house and maneuvered his silver 2003 Lexus onto I-5 for the drive to the Commish's El Cajon mansion.

When Bob arrived at Bernie's house at around 2:30 P.M., he noted with satisfaction the absence of Ladies' Man at his customary station at the front door handing out invoices to collect his side bet winnings. This was not L-Man's year. It was Buckeye's time to collect.

Bob ducked around back, where he found Ladies' Man entertaining the Commish's babysitter with witty anecdotes.

"Yo, Ladies' Man."

"Yo, Bob. What's happenin'?"

"I got a little something for you."

Bob took out a crisp white envelope and handed it to Ladies' Man, who took it as if it had anthrax in it.

"What's this? A subpoena for child support?"

"No. It's your invoice for the side bets. I take major credit cards and wire transfers."

"Shee-it, Bob. You've hit the big time now."

Inside the Commish's mansion, the Commish collected money from everyone ages eight to eighty. Over the years, he had developed several games of chance based on the Super Bowl. Today, he administered ten different bets ranging from simple to complex. He most liked the betting square game. For a meager ten dollars per square, participants would receive a random square on a grid corresponding to the number of points scored by each team at the end of a given quarter. Ladies' Man normally bought ten of the one hundred squares for a hundred dollar entry fee.

The other side bets required guessing:

- The player who would score the first touchdown
- The length of the first field goal
- How many Bud Light commercials would be aired during the Super Bowl
- Who would make the first tackle of the game
- Which team would get the first penalty
- Who would throw the red challenge flag first
- How many total points would be scored in the game
- Which team would make the first turnover

While the gambling festivities proceeded, a few party goers busied themselves raiding the ample buffet of corn chips, salsa, guacamole, pizza, ribs, chicken, brownies, and cookies. Others gathered around the big screen TV in the living room, watching the pregame broadcast and keeping an eye out for the new crop of special Super Bowl commercials. In an adjacent room, a dozen or so children of various ages played with a large pile of toys and watched videos, contained and preoccupied at least for the moment.

Just as the pregame show concluded and the kickoff neared, the Commish gathered up the group, took hold of the remote, and dialed down the volume. He held the BIGFFL trophy in his other hand.

"Can I have everyone's attention, please? As most of you know, it is customary to hand out the BIGFFL championship trophy before the opening kickoff. This year, the trophy goes to a first-time recipient, Buckeye Bob DiGiorgio. Congratulations, Bob."

Bob came up and grasped the trophy, holding it up with two hands and kissing it like a U.S. Open champion. Everyone applauded, and the crowd punctuated the air with, "Way to go, Bob!"

Marty remained by himself, the only one unhappy for Bob. He hadn't gotten over his loss, because, with Bob's victory, the ultracompetitive Tanaka had become the only owner never to have won the championship. Instead of mixing with the others during the trophy presentation, he seethed on the patio.

After the award ceremony, Bob wasted no time enjoying his pimping rights, making the rounds while everyone else watched the Super Bowl.

"Nice going, Bob. Great season."

"Thanks, Exacta. I'm thinking repeat next season. Care to wager?"

"You know me. I never turn down a good bet."

"How about you, Junk? You want a piece of the action."

"Let me get this straight. You win once in fifteen seasons, and now you're talkin' repeat? I'll definitely put my money down on that. Here's fifty bucks. We'll get Commish to set the odds. Hey, Commish, we need your help, in an official capacity."

The Commish finished his pastrami sandwich, grabbed his beer, and came over.

"What can I do for you, gentlemen?"

"Bob here is laying down bets on a second championship in a row next season. We need some odds."

The Commish pondered for a moment.

"Let's put it at forty-five to one. Sorry, Bob, but you're still a long shot. You win again, and maybe the odds'll come down."

"No problem, Commish. More money for me when I win. I beefed up the memory on my computer and added two additional parameters to refine my draft program. I can't lose."

"That's great, Bob."

As everyone handed in their money to Ladies' Man, Marty approached Bob.

"Hey, Marty. How's it goin'? Tough luck this year, huh?"

"You ain't shittin', Bob. Especially to lose to a sorry SOB like you. Winning with your lineup is kind of the equivalent of Poland beating the United States in a war. In fact, on top of my hundred that I'm puttin' down on this bet, I got two hundred more says you finish dead last next year."

"You're on, Cactus. And I've got another two hundred that says you do the same."

"Ain't gonna happen, Bob. Ain't gonna happen. This time next year, I'll have that trophy. You watch."

Marty scowled as he wandered out to the patio for another beer. Bob just laughed, basking in the championship glory. Chet, who had been listening, came over to Bob. "Hey, Bob, what's with the Cactus Man? Pretty poor loser."

"Nah, he's okay. I'd be steamed too if I was the only guy *never* to win a championship."

They both got a good laugh out of that.

While everyone talked, laughed, and caught up with each other, the game itself had the makings of one of the better ones in the history of the Super Bowl. The Patriots and the Eagles played each other very close, and at the end of the first quarter, they had deadlocked 0–0.

Double zeros rarely won because of the unlikely combination. As the Commish consulted the scoring grid and located the square coinciding with 0–0, he saw Buckeye Bob's name. He grabbed the cash and walked over to Bob, interrupting his needling of Exacta.

"Hey, Bob, you won the first quarter square. Here're your winnings."

"I tell ya, this is the start of something big. I feel like Superman right now."

The game continued to be very tight, tied at 7–7 at half time. Once again, Bob drew the magic square, taking the prize. After distributing the winnings again, the Commish summoned the group together for some traditional Super Bowl party events, including a putting contest and a bit of touch football in the backyard.

"As you all know, the backyard is pretty small and there's a steep drop-off on the right sideline, so the teams are three on three. We'll have the putting contest at the same time, and we'll rotate players into the football when they're not putting."

The partygoers enjoyed the spectacle of a bunch of middle-aged men playing touch football on a twenty-yard by twenty-yard patch of grass, struggling to stay in the field of play without tumbling down the steep bank, hearing the groans and labored breathing, and smelling the tang of sweat. Fortunately, all the participants opted to leave their shirts on, sparing spectators the spectacle of seas of white flab.

When the dust settled, team A beat team B 14–7, and as a small consolation prize, Marty Tanaka won the putting contest, which was held on a small strip of Astroturf leading to an elevated plastic cup. Still, it took a playoff with Buckeye Bob for Marty to take the contest. As Marty sunk the last putt to clinch, he did a bizarre victory dance akin to *Young Frankenstein's* "Puttin' on the Ritz" and decided to assert some pimping rights of his own.

"Hey, Bob, nice try, but this is a sign of things to come. I am going to clean your clock next year and take all your cash. You can bet on it."

Buckeye Bob contemplated for a moment, deep in thought. He smiled and patted Marty on the shoulder.

"That's okay, Marty. Everyone's gotta have something to hold onto. You might want to remember this moment, because it's probably the last chance you'll have to savor a win."

The game continued neck and neck, until the Patriots edged the Eagles out 24–21. Usually when the final gun sounded, the place had pretty well cleared out, but this year the game had everyone riveted to the TV.

"Wow, what a game! Well, since I have everyone here still, I get to give out the winnings in person for a change. In a disturbing trend that we hope won't continue next year, the developing Buckeye Bob dynasty has taken player scoring the first touchdown, Smith from the Eagles—"

Junkyard piped up, "That was a lucky catch."

"It's *all* luck, Junk. Anyway, Bob also took the length of the first field goal, twenty-two yards, total points, forty-five, and who would make the first turnover, the Eagles. All told, I think Bob netted around $345. Nice going, Bob."

The Commish handed over a wad of bills to Bob, who took the opportunity to wave it under Marty's nose.

"For the rest, Exacta got first tackle of the game, New England. Mrs. Commish got first penalty, New England. Pat Rollins picked up who would throw the red challenge flag first. And no one got the number of Bud Light commercials because I lost track of how many they aired. I will do some research and get back to you on that. Anyway, thanks for coming. Until next year!"

Mr. and Mrs. Commish greeted everyone at the door as they left. Some people kept on partying, including L-Man, who was once again playing one-on-one with Gail the babysitter.

"Take care, Marty. Better luck next year."

"Luck won't have nothing to do with it."

"Whatever that means. See ya, Bob. Don't spend all your loot in one place."

"Nah. It's all going to computer bandwidth, research materials, and dog biscuits. Well, thanks for another great Super Bowl party Commish, Mrs. Commish."

"Pleasure as always, Bob. Drive carefully."

Bob set down the trophy in the back seat of his Lexus, securing it with the seat belt, got into the car, balancing himself to accommodate the bulge in his wallet and took the winding hill down from the Commish's house. He floated on air as he savored his victory, already starting to think about next year.

The Commish and Ladies' Man were reclined on the Commish's back patio overlooking Willow Glen Drive and debating the relative merit of Super Bowl commercials when the Commish noticed an erratic Bud truck in the fading light.

"Hey, L-Man, that truck looks like it's going to hit something."

"Isn't that Bob's car?"

"Holy shit."

They saw the Bud truck correct its course and drive past while a maroon Chevy truck collided with Bob's Lexus. Bob's car looked like a toy as it careened back and forth, ending up about forty feet from its original position.

The Commish dashed around the side of the house to his car. Ladies' Man followed.

"Call 911!" Ladies' Man shouted to the other partygoers as he passed the open kitchen window.

When they arrived at the accident, they sprinted to Bob's car and carefully extricated him from the wreckage. Bob had suffered a blow to the head and had no pulse. While the Commish administered CPR, Ladies' Man met the first wave of assistance, including two police cars and two ambulances staffed with paramedics. Ladies' Man waved over the first pair of paramedics, explained the situation, and gestured in Bob's direction. The paramedics rushed to Bob's side.

The two backed away from the paramedics as they began to work on Bob. In a daze, they wandered over to the curb and sat down. A short time later, one of the paramedics approached them. The Commish got to his feet.

"We did everything we could. The head trauma was too severe. Do you know how we can reach his next of kin?"

After the paramedic walked off, the Commish sat back down with Ladies' Man and patted him on the shoulder. Together, they stared into the black hillside.

POSTGAME SHOW

On yet another typical San Diego day in early February, the sun was bright, not a cloud in the sky, and it was unseasonably warm. All of the denizens of the BIGFFL, friends for so long, gathered at the First Orthodox Catholic Church for a sad, somber moment: the farewell to Buckeye Bob.

As his fellow BIGFFLers gathered around the open casket— CSFBIM, Junkyard Dog, Exacta, Slowhand, Ladies' Man, Cactus Connection, and Gregory and Son—everyone admired the way the caretaker had dressed Bob. He lay in his sleek, mahogany, silk-lined coffin dressed in his brown pants and orange polo shirt in honor of the Cleveland Browns. To the side of the casket, on a small table, sat the BIGFFL trophy and the photo from this year's Perfect Day. Bob had that big smile on his face.

As each of them waited to view the body and say their own private farewells, they talked among themselves. Only Marty Tanaka stood off to the side, still angered by his last minute defeat.

"What's up with Marty?" asked the Ladies' Man.

"Oh, he's still pissed off that Bob won the championship this year. He still hasn't gotten over it." Slowhand shook his head in disbelief.

Chet looked over at Tanaka, worried about his current state, and remarked, "Wow, he looks pretty amped. You sure he's okay?"

Junk chuckled, "What's he gonna do, rush the casket?"

Ladies' Man paid his respects first. "Hey, Bob, congratulations on such a great year. What a way to go out, huh? Anyway, here's the money I owe you." He proceeded to place a one hundred dollar bill in Bob's coffin, looking left and right to make sure no one noticed. "Rest in peace."

Chet Russell approached next.

"Say, Bob, sorry about all those times we took advantage of you with those bad trades. We couldn't help ourselves. Anyway, it all turned out for the best, didn't it? We're gonna miss you, man. Take care."

All this time, Marty brooded in the corner, turning redder and redder. The Commish noticed him first as he bolted toward the table next to the coffin.

"Marty!"

Marty sprinted toward the trophy, screaming as he went.

"That's my trophy, you son-of-a-bitch! Who the hell takes Attoi Roi and the entire Browns lineup and then WINS with them? I want my trophy!"

A wall of BIGFFLers met Marty before he got anywhere near the trophy. As a group, they hoisted him into the air and carried him outside to calm him down. They appointed Slowhand to take him away and keep an eye on him until he composed himself enough to return. With disaster averted, they returned to the service.

After everyone paid their respects and sat down, Ladies' Man got up to give the eulogy.

"Friends and loved ones of Robert T. DiGiorgio, what can I say about one of my best friends and one of the greatest guys you'd ever wanna meet? Bob was like a brother to me. He was generous and kind, always willing to help out someone else in need. I thought about what I could say about Bob to do him justice, and I really struggled, because I didn't want to overdo it. So I decided to focus on the incredible fantasy football season he had this year.

"I remember going back fifteen years to the first season we had. Bob was always working the hardest of any of us trying to set his draft strategy and succeed in the league. Until this year, he was always at the bottom of the standings. All that hard work finally paid off, although no one would have thought it when we saw his team after the draft. Week after week, as things went his way, you could just see the joy in his eyes, his confidence growing. And the miracle finally came to pass. He won it all.

"He was so young, but you know the old saying 'When it's time to go … go in style!' Bob certainly did that. He left us on top!

"My sincerest condolences to Bob's lovely wife and our good friend Rachel, as well as Bob's family and friends. We will really miss Buckeye Bob."

Ladies' Man wiped a tear from his eye as he came down from the podium, slipping his speech into his jacket pocket. As they filed out of the church, the Commish slapped Ladies' Man on the back.

"Hang in there, buddy. Rachel needs us right now."

The next morning, a massive group assembled at the church to pay their final respects to Bob. They came from all walks of life, and some had not seen Bob in thirty years. Childhood friends from his old neighborhood in Cleveland. George Stuart, his Little League coach. Mrs. Daugherty, his high school English teacher. All his old friends from North & Sullivan.

After the priest blessed the casket, the burial party boarded hearses for the slow ride to the Heavenly Meadows Cemetery, followed by a long procession of cars. As the Commish and Ladies' Man escorted Rachel to the lead hearse, the driver stepped forward.

"Sorry for your loss. I'm Frank, your driver. Lemme get the door for you."

Frank, a short, stocky guy with bright red hair shooting out from under his chauffeur's hat, had large eyes streaked with red, and he smelled of gin. His most memorable feature, a huge bushy moustache, reminded one of the professional golfer Craig "Walrus" Stadler. A small smear of mustard cut a swath across his right lapel, marring an otherwise immaculate black suit.

The Commish and Ladies' Man nodded to Frank and entered the limo, joining Rachel in the back. She looked lovely, her beautiful features softened by her sadness and grief. Her black hair curved under her chin, framing her tanned, youthful face. She wore a subdued shade of mauve lipstick and very little makeup. A few tears escaped from her brownish green eyes as she daubed them with a rumpled Kleenex.

"Thank you both for being so wonderful and staying with me. I don't know what I would do without you."

"We're glad to do it, Rachel."

Frank took up his position in the driver's seat and addressed his passengers through the open window separating the front and the back of the hearse.

"Folks, we'll be starting out in about five minutes. Once we do, the drive should take about thirty minutes, give or take. En route, please help yourself to food and beverage if you want. We have a fully stocked refrigerator and bar. Just let me know if there's anything I can do."

While Frank gave his little speech, the Ladies' Man checked out the bar.

"Hey Commish, Frank here is right. The bar is very nicely stocked. I think we should have a drink in Bob's honor. Rachel, you want anything?"

"Robert, I don't think she—"

But Rachel cut him off in midsentence. "Sure, Robert. Can you fix me a martini, extra dry, three olives? It'll calm my nerves."

"One of my favorites," Frank chimed in from the front.

"No problem, Rach. Comin' right up. While I'm at it, I think I'll make myself one. Sure I can't get you anything, Commish?"

"No thanks, Robert. Someone's gotta watch the ship."

"Suit yourself, Commish. How about you, Frank? You want anything to prep you for the drive?"

"I thought you'd never ask. I'll take a super dry martini with two olives."

The Ladies' Man ignored Frank's request and got to work making the drinks.

Once they all settled in, drinks in hand, Frank started up the hearse and made his way out of the church parking lot toward the main road.

"Man, Commish, I don't know why, but for some reason, these hearses remind me of the good old days when we used to take limos to the races for the Perfect Day. That was sweet. Why don't we do that anymore?"

A flashing montage of good times went through Bernie's head, the Perfect Days past with the group, the camaraderie and fun they had experienced over the past fifteen years.

"Yeah, I remember that like it was yesterday. The best of times."

The hearse grew silent, as they each stared out the windows, taking a brief stroll down memory lane on the drive to the cemetery.

The hearses and cars all arrived at Heavenly Meadows, depositing the friends and family of Bob DiGiorgio. Everyone gathered around the open grave. The Roman Catholic priest, an elderly Italian, said his final words. "And we commit our friend in Christ, Bob DiGiorgio, to the earth and to the Heavenly Father's infinite glory and love. Amen."

As they lowered the coffin into the ground, Rachel looked on as each person approached the grave, tossing in a handful of dirt or a flower as they said good-bye. One of the last to pay his respects, the Commish stood over the grave with a copy of the photo of the last Perfect Day group taken behind the eighteenth green clutched in his hands.

"Hey, Bob, here's a little memento to take with you, you know, to remember everyone by. When you get to heaven, have it framed or something."

He let go of the photo and it floated down, landing face up on the casket. Bob's face smiled up from the middle of the picture. The Commish turned away from the grave with reluctance and headed toward the hearse.

After Rachel spent some last moments at the grave, Ladies' Man said his good-byes. Fighting back tears, he stood over the grave with the BIGFFL championship trophy.

"You know, Bob, the league's not going to be the same without you. I have so many memorable moments. Like the time we kicked some golfing ass in Vegas and won all the cash. And the multiple times you chose Bernie Kosar as your first pick in the draft. And the time you had to spend most of the season working in Reno, drunk off your ass. I couldn't believe you never changed your lineup. By the time the season was over, you only had two active players. Geez, one of your players was actually dead, and one was in prison.

"It's been great having you as a friend. We'll look out for Rachel for you and, if you get a chance, pay us a visit sometime. Hell, maybe we'll hold a séance and see if we can get you to join us. Anyway, good-bye Bob. And before I go, there's one more thing I want to do. I want you to have this."

Ladies' Man held the trophy over the grave and let it fall. It landed next to the photo.

"Hold onto that, and treasure it. You earned it!"

As Ladies' Man backed away from the grave, giving Bob the thumbs up, he noticed Bob's tombstone, which said:

Here lies Bob DiGiorgio
Beloved husband to Rachel
And Champion of BIGFFL XV

Born 1960
Died 2005

As he read the tombstone, Ladies' Man caught movement out of the corner of his eye. Outside the black wrought iron fence of the cemetery stretched a large county park, the lush green grass glowing in the afternoon sun. A father and his son, no more than six years old, played catch with a football. The father spoke to his son, telling him how to throw a spiral. The son listened, nodding his head and making throwing gestures with his arm. His father tossed him the ball and, lo and behold, the kid threw a perfect spiral, jumping up and down and laughing, the future golden before him.

"That kid's the next Brett Favre."

Ladies' Man smiled to himself and began his walk to the hearse.

MONDAY MORNING QUARTERBACK

Buckeye Bob stood in line, staring down through an opening in billowy white clouds at his funeral.

"Hot damn! They gave me the trophy after all."

He pumped his fist and turned to the person in front of him, Hunter S. Thompson. Thompson removed a cigarette from his mouth and stared at Bob through dark sunglasses.

"There are only two types of people in this world, the doomed and screwheads. Nixon was a screwhead. Which one are you?"

Bob had no answer, so he turned to the person behind him, the king of late night TV, Johnny Carson, who was in the middle of his patented Karnak routine. He had an envelope held up to his head in mock consideration. He gave the envelope to one of his audience, who opened it and gave the answer, "Touchback."

Carson thought briefly and provided the question, "What's the smart thing to do if a Dallas Cowgirl touches you?"

As Bob moved forward, he looked down to see that he was walking on a football field, moving toward a goal line and end zone. Beyond the end zone and wrapping around him, he saw Municipal Stadium. When Bob got to the five yard line, Otto Graham, the prototype Hall of Fame Browns quarterback, silently handed him an official NFL football and Bob proceeded to cross the goal line.

Not quite sure what to do, Bob spiked the ball and a crowd appeared in the bleachers, roaring their approval and chanting, "Buck-Eye-Bob! Buck-Eye-Bob!" Turning to his left, he noticed Paul Brown approaching him.

"Congratulations, son. You scored the winning touchdown. We would like to award you with this trophy as a token of your victory."

It was the BIGFFL trophy. Bob held it up, and the crowd let out a deafening roar. When he was done, Brown patted him on the shoulder.

"Son, you've worked hard. It's time for you to hit the showers. They're that way."

Brown pointed toward the tunnel entrance, and Bob followed. As he neared the tunnel, he looked up and noticed a gold sign that said "Pearly Gates." As he made his final trek up the tunnel, he savored the approval of the crowd until it gradually diminished to quiet.

APPENDIX 1

Championship Teams by Season

1990 Ladies' Man
1991 Junkyard Dog
1992 CSFBIM
1993 Ladies' Man
1994 Exacta
1995 Gregory
1996 Slowhand
1997 CSFBIM
1998 Gregory
1999 Ladies' Man
2000 Slowhand
2001 Ladies' Man
2002 CSFBIM
2003 Gregory & Son
2004 Buckeye Bob

APPENDIX 2

Cumulative Won/Loss Records
and Percentages by Team

TEAM	Wins	Losses	Percentage
Ladies' Man	159	81	66%
CSFBIM	148	92	62%
Gregory (& Son)	147	93	61%
Junkyard Dog	121	119	50%
Slowhand	113	127	47%
Exacta	96	144	40%
Cactus Connection	94	146	39%
Buckeye Bob	82	158	34%

Printed in the United States
129594LV00002B/43-138/P

9 780595 506767